THE THIEF

Amanda Michelle Moon

Spiraling Forward Press
amanda@spiralingforward.com
www.spiralingforward.com

Ordering Information:
Quantity sales. Special discounts are available on quantity purchases by corporations, associations, and others. For details, contact the publisher at the address above.

Printed in the United States of America

ISBN
Softcover: 978-1-943250-01-1
ePub: 978-0-9903326-2-6
Mobi: 978-0-9903326-1-9
1st Edition Softcover: 978-0-9903326-0-2

Second Edition
Cover Photo by Chris Evans.

For Christopher, Lily and Austin

THE
THIEF

AMANDA MICHELLE MOON

ONE

I wait until I can't see or hear any cars on the highway, take a deep breath, and swing the crowbar. There is a resounding thud as metal hits glass. Then—stillness. I raise the crowbar again, but before I can swing a second time, the glass cracks. Spider webbing. And, finally, it shatters, raining down onto the linoleum floor inside the Judy Garland Museum in Grand Rapids, Minnesota.

I am wearing all black except for the tinted glasses covering the eye-holes of my face mask. I tested several different colored lenses to be sure I would be able to see inside the dark museum but be unrecognizable on the cameras. Red worked best. Fun, since I'm stealing the red shoes.

I reach through the broken window and press the crash bar to unlatch the door, then pull it open from the outside. I count to ten, listening for sirens. I know there is an alarm, but I only hear silence. I step through, one foot at a time, onto the yellow floor. Glass crunches under my feet. I pause again, in case the alarm is motion triggered.

Nothing.

I take one long, deep breath and my heart rate begins to return to normal. Either the alarm is silent or it's broken; either way, I'm inside. I've been here before, so I know exactly where to go and what to do. It takes two long strides to get to the door that leads from this hallway to the main museum. I reach for the handle with my left hand, crowbar in the right, ready to shatter the narrow window if necessary.

It pulls easily. No lock.

Inside the museum the floor is beige linoleum with white squares every few feet. The walls on one side are lined with framed pictures, letters, and crap that covers Judy Garland's life basically from birth until she killed herself. On the other side, and in the middle, are eight-foot tall glass cases of memorabilia: costumes, movie props, awards. Directly in front of me is the carriage that carried Judy, the Tin Man, the Scarecrow, and Lion into the Emerald City in *The Wizard of Oz*.

The shoes stand on a white wooden podium in the middle of the room, enclosed in a square, glass case. They are sitting on a piece of yellow fabric, to remind you that they walked the Yellow Brick Road. The glass is screwed to the podium on all four sides, and a large black sign announces *Dorothy's Ruby Slippers* in white and red lettering.

I swing the crowbar like a bat, making sure to aim high enough not to damage the shoes. This time the glass shatters immediately and goes flying everywhere.

Grabbing the shoes, I hold my breath again. There has to be an alarm on the actual podium.

Silence.

This is way too easy.

I gently shake the glass out of the shoes. In six steps I am back in the hallway. I laugh when I see the sign on the door: "EMERGENCY EXIT ONLY. ALARM WILL SOUND." I push the crash bar and I'm out into the Minnesota night.

A stand of evergreen trees lines the walk between the main museum and The Birthplace Museum, the house that Judy Garland grew up in. It provides enough shelter for me to stop, wrap the shoes carefully in a towel, and put them in my backpack. I listen again for any sounds of alarm, or sirens. There has to be an alarm, even if it is silent. Someone should know by now. I don't want to leave until I know which direction the cop cars are coming from.

The night is warm. Stars blanket the sky.

The adrenaline is kicking in. My hands are shaking as I pull off my gloves. There are tiny little pieces of orange-red felt stuck to my clothes that I can't seem to brush off. My sweaty palm barely moves them, and there are too many to stand here and pick at individually. I'm not worried; the hard part is over. I can get rid of the clothes.

I did it.

I have THE RUBY SLIPPERS. One of the most valuable pieces of Hollywood memorabilia is in my backpack.

And it was easy. Maybe too easy. There is a tiny hint of worry trying to work its way into my brain, but I ignore it and light a cigarette. The nicotine calms my nerves, steadies my hands. There are still no sirens. Maybe this is one of those places that puts up all of the signs but doesn't actually have a security system. Maybe I don't have anything to worry about.

There is so much more in the museum. Awards. Costumes. Stuff I might actually be able to sell. To not only get out of the fucking hole my life is stuck in, but to climb the ladder a little bit.

I'm going back in.

I put my cigarette out on the sole of my shoe and tuck the butt in my pocket. No evidence. And I can finish it later. I hoist my backpack to my shoulders, the crowbar sticking out and slightly hooked over my head, and go back to the door. My hand is on the crash bar when I hear it.

In the distance, the long honk of a semi, and sirens.

I hesitate and my heart rate picks up again. Maybe they are going to the hospital. I might still have time.

I pull the door open and have one foot inside. But the sirens are close enough now that the sounds are echoing in the hallway. I've got the shoes. I can't get caught because I'm being greedy.

I slam the door and run, not bothering to see whether it latches.

There are two hotels beside the museum, a national chain right next door and a local landmark a little further down. I'm parked where the two lots meet, back with the other trucks and boats. I stay in the tree line to avoid being seen by anyone on the highway and I run until I'm behind The Sawmill Inn, the local hotel. There is a couple— the man, stumbling drunk, his arm around the shoulders of a much-smaller woman trying to hold him up— wandering around the parking lot, looking for their car. He's singing a country song at the top of his lungs; she's giggling. He leans down to kiss her. They wouldn't remember me even if they do see me, and being here when the cops arrive isn't an option.. I'm just about ready to bolt to my truck when they turn toward the larger vehicles in the back of the lot.

"Hey!" he yells. "There it is!" He lets go of her and runs toward me, veering. I slowly back into the trees, hoping he hasn't already seen me. He stops, bends over and rests his hands on his knees. "Woo hoo!" He stands up and pumps his fists. He's scanning the parking lot, the trees, for anyone to celebrate with him. And his eyes lock on mine.

He can't see me.

There is no way he can see me.

But he's looking straight at me.

The woman catches up with him, puts her arm around his waist and gently turns him. His head jerks around, still scanning the lot, looking for something, but his eyes don't stop on me again. She leads him to a white pickup and shoves him in the passenger's seat, then runs around to the driver's seat and climbs in. She backs out and, for a moment, the headlights illuminate the front of the evergreen stand. But she doesn't look up. He's already asleep.

The sirens have disappeared. They weren't coming for me after all. I dig the cigarette out of my pocket and wait long after the truck is gone before moving.

I think again about going back into the museum, but I've got what I came for. It would be stupid to get greedy now. I know I left no trace at the scene. Even if the man saw me, and remembers it tomorrow, no one will believe him. I finish the cigarette and shove the butt back into my pocket, then pick my way carefully down the small hill onto the asphalt. I walk calmly to my truck, gently laying the backpack in the passenger's seat.

Back at my apartment I pull a beer out of the fridge, sit in the worn leather recliner, and turn on the TV.

I go to sleep and dream of skipping down a yellow brick road.

TWO

I wake up at ten forty-five, pissed. I wanted to see the morning news. I need to know what they are saying. I flip around the local channels, in case coverage of the Great Heist is preempting any of the morning talk shows.

It's not.

In my room, I take off my black clothes and have to smell shirts to figure out which piles of laundry on the floor are clean and which are dirty. I find a decent smelling pair of jeans and a blue t-shirt to put on, and grab my Tar Heels hat.

My backpack is on the counter in the kitchen. I open it, wanting to pull the shoes out and hold them, revel in my triumph. For just a moment. When I picked them up last night they were much flimsier than I had expected. There are still tiny pieces of felt clinging to the hair on my arms. I pull the towel back to look at them. The "rubies" are just sequins that have somehow been sewn on. Sewn a million years ago when the movie was made. The thin threads look like the slightest touch could cause the entire shoe to fall apart. The big jewels on the tops of the shoes look like the kind of beads you give to little kids for art projects. And there are clumps of glue, old and brown, around their edges, like they had to keep re-gluing them during the filming. I gently tuck the towel back around the shoes and close the backpack.

I will take very good care of them for the little time I'll have them with me. They're my ticket. This whole life, with all of its problems— the gambling, the debt, the drugs, everything, it's all going to be behind me. Gone. I want to call my parents. To tell them they don't have to worry about me anymore. I've finally got my shit together. I'll be able to come home soon.

I pick up my phone, my fingers hover over the numbers. I can't call them. Not yet. I have to wait until this is done. I don't want to jinx it. Maybe I'll surprise them at Christmas. That would be awesome. Just show up at their house. Finally safe, clean. Finally their son again.

I put the phone back on the table and go to the bathroom to brush my teeth. The museum should be open by now. I need to know what's going on. I look at my reflection in the mirror, wanting to see the change in my face. Instead of being tinged in red, my eyes are clear and bright. The muscles in my arms and chest are well defined, and I'm tan. I'm healthy. It feels good. I smile. I'm starting to look more and more like my dad. Same straight brown hair, same brown/green eyes.

I hesitate in the kitchen, weighing the risks of taking the shoes versus leaving them here. I wouldn't be taking them back to the scene of the crime, exactly. There's a restaurant in the Sawmill Inn, where I parked my truck last night. Putting it back in the same lot wouldn't draw any suspicion; people will assume I'm staying there. I can get some food and see what people are saying.

But I can't take the backpack. It's too much. Too risky. I have to be smart this time.

I put the bag in the corner of my bedroom closet and kick dirty clothes in around it. There is a semi-nice grey jacket hanging on the back of my door; I grab it and my keys, making sure to double-check that the door is locked when I leave.

In the truck I scan radio stations until I finally find the news.

"Developing story out of Itasca County today. Grand Rapids is reeling after the discovery this morning that the famed Ruby Slippers were stolen from the Judy Garland Museum overnight. The Slippers, one of five pairs worn by Garland in The Wizard of Oz, *were on loan from a collector and scheduled to go back to California next week. Police are investigating all leads. If anyone has any information, you are asked to contact the Grand Rapids Police Department. In other news, Hurricane Katrina is closing in on the Gulf*

Shore. Residents of Florida, Mississippi, Alabama and Louisiana have all received evacuation orders."

The news program continued to talk about the hurricane with weather guys debating whether or not this was going to be "the big one."

I check my phone.

He hasn't called.

I want to call him. To tell him I have the shoes. But I can't. The Senator, as he likes to be called, hadn't given me his real name, much less a contact phone number.

But I'm surprised Joey hasn't called either.

*****

The Judy Garland Museum is on Highway 169 on the south end of Grand Rapids, one of the first sights to welcome tourists coming up from the Twin Cities. Coming from the north, though, I can't see anything from the road. I debate driving past the museum, but there isn't a good place to turn around further south. Instead, I pull up the little hill into the hotel parking lot and drive more slowly than is necessary to survey the situation. There isn't much to see— just a few police cars and a small group of people standing on the grass between the Country Inn and the museum.

A car behind me honks, a polite *honk-honk* to let me know he needs to get by, and I gun it to the back of the lot. I park my truck in the same area where it was last night, but it's more exposed now. A lot of the trucks with boats aren't in the lot; they're probably out fishing.

I get out of my truck and slowly walk toward the museum and the crowd on the grass. I know it's stupid. But I have to know what's going on. What they've found. What they think they know. The dog-days sun is burning brightly in the sky, and I keep my hat pulled low and my sunglasses— my normal ones, not the red ones— on to cover my eyes.

There are only three police cars. I expected more. The museum didn't even open until ten. I don't know what time the staff got in, or when they discovered the shattered glass or the missing shoes. But I thought there would be more activity. I pictured crime scene investigators, like on television, taking pictures, crawling on the ground, looking for forensic evidence. I smile thinking about them trying to get DNA samples from every piece of fuzz and hair on the floor inside.

I know I left nothing.

"What's going on?" I ask the man next to me, trying to make my voice deeper than normal. The crowd is mostly senior citizens, couples that are probably here for brunch after church.

"Oh, some yahoo went and stole the Ruby Slippers last night," he says. He looks to be in his mid-sixties and is wearing a red flannel shirt even though it's nearly seventy degrees already.

"Do they know who did it?"

"I think one of them crazy fans probably took 'em," a different man says.

"Nah, I bet it was someone from around here," said another.

"No one around here would do that," one of the women says.

"Yeah, they're all too busy worrying about getting in the last bit of fishing before the summer's over," another lady says, and everyone laughs. The conversation quickly turns to the best lakes to catch northern pike and bass now and who is taking more than the legal limit of crappies.

I quietly back out of the crowd. I'm tempted to see if I can get any closer, to see what is really going on, but even I have my limits. Instead, I pretend to be walking to a truck in the back of the Country Inn parking lot, checking for activity behind the museum. There is one investigator walking around, looking at the ground, and I feel a jolt of panic. What if he finds prints from my boots? What if he somehow lifts my fingerprints from the tree bark? I hold my breath, watching him, but he stays close to the back door, eventually shaking his head and walking away, rounding the far corner of the building. I go the opposite direction, away from the museum to The Sawmill.

I can see the dining room is packed, as usual, as I approach the hostess stand.

"Table for one?"

"Do you have a reservation?" She's young, probably still in high school. Her blond hair is pulled back in a tight ponytail, her white uniform shirt tucked into very, very low-rise black pants. I expect her to pop her gum.

"No."

She sighs and picks up her pen. "Your name?

"Jared Canning."

"I can try to squeeze you in, but there's going to be a wait. Reservations are highly recommended, even for a party of one."

I nod. "Thank you."

"You can wait out here." She turns to the family behind me before I even move away from the podium. They had reservations; their table for twelve is ready.

The hotel lobby smells like heat and chlorine. Tourists are milling around on brown leather chairs, leaning against the log-sided walls, standing in large groups, all talking too loudly for Sunday morning. Kids in dripping swim suits run back and forth from the pool off one side of the lobby to the arcade off the other, occasionally finding their parents to ask for money. I follow the trail of water to the vending machines and get a Mountain Dew, then find a seat in the middle of the room. I'm glad I grabbed the jacket. It's too hot for it, but I look nicer; it helps me blend in better. I do my best to filter through the conversations, to listen without turning my head toward any particular speakers, and to remain inconspicuous.

"...I don't know. Well it's just terrible. Who would do..."

"...They are saying the alarms weren't turned on. It had to have been an inside job. Where was the security..."

"...I bet it was a set-up. Insurance money. Those shoes are probably worth more gone..."

"…It's just so sad. Nothing like this ever happens here. It's such a quiet town…"

The bit about the inside job and the insurance are interesting theories. It is good to know the investigation is being directed somewhere already, and that it isn't pointing anywhere near me.

THREE

The local television station's *News at Noon* is running basically the same story I had heard on the radio, although they have a reporter live on the scene. For a moment I wish I had stuck around long enough to see the news crew arrive, but as the story goes on, punctuated by pictures of the Slippers and the inside of the museum, I realize it doesn't matter. They don't know anything.

I pull a beer out of the fridge and extend the legs on my recliner. It was a long night. I'm tired.

I check my phone one last time— still no calls from Joey or The Senator.

The news ends and a NASCAR race comes on. The sound of the engines, rhythmically running around the track, lulls me to sleep. My dreams are disjointed; first I'm driving a race car, then I'm being chased by one, then I'm being chased by the cops, sirens blaring. Then the noise changes into the "Breaking News" theme that all of the networks use to interrupt regular programing. The music stops and I hear:

"We interrupt this broadcast to bring you breaking news…"

I jolt awake, realizing what I'm hearing is real.

I jerk the lever to bring the end of my chair down and my feet crash to the floor. I grab the remote and turn the volume up, waiting for the station information to clear and the anchor to come on.

National news! A jolt of adrenaline shoots through me. This is it. I lean to see out the window. There are no cops outside. They must be going national with it, looking for clues.

I'm good.

The graphic clears, and the screen changes to a newsroom where a middle aged man with a full head of greying hair sits behind a desk, the "Breaking News!" logo on a screen behind him.

"We're sorry to interrupt your programing, but we've got breaking news out of Louisiana."

What? Louisiana?

"New Orleans Mayor Ray Nagin has declared a state of emergency and is ordering a mandatory evacuation of the city. Hurricane Katrina has been upgraded to a category five storm and is currently gathering strength off the Gulf Coast. It is expected to make landfall early tomorrow morning with

catastrophic consequences. The last time a storm of this size…"

They are showing rows of cars and buses lined up as people evacuate the coast. I get up to take a leak and half listen as they play interviews with people refusing to leave.

"I've lived here all my life. If this is the big one, bring it on."

"We don't have anywhere to go. This happens every year and we spend so much money on travel and hotels. We're just going to ride it out this year."

I am zipping my pants when I hear his voice. I run back into the living room, holding my still-open pants with one hand.

"You know," the Senator is saying, smiling into the camera, "I think I'm pretty safe here. We've got the windows boarded and the house secure. We've got a few days' food and water, some good movies, and, if we lose power, books and candles. We'll be just fine."

I sit back in my chair. I've never seen him before. We've just spoken on the phone once. His voice, the deep, Barry White baritone, had painted an entirely different picture in my head. I thought he was a big, burly guy. Maybe black, I didn't know for sure. Definitely not this five-foot five-inch Mr. Rogers type in a cardigan and bow tie. His sandy-blond hair blows lightly in the wind. There is no name caption on his picture.

I pick up my phone. Still no calls.
Fuck it. I dial Joey.

"What the hell, man?" I ask when he answers the phone.

His normally gruff voice is raspy.

"Are you still sleeping?"

He mumbles something I can't understand.

"What the fuck? I've been waiting for you all day and you're still sleeping?

"Calm down," he croaks. "It was a long night."

"Really? Tell me about it. What did you do last night?"

"Shut the fuck up, man. Did you get them?"

"Of course I got them. And I want to get rid of them." I take a deep breath. I can't get Joey upset. If this deal falls through… I can't have stolen them for nothing.

"Patience. Let me call and see where The Senator is."

"I know where he is. I just saw him on TV."

"What?"

"TV. He's on the news. He's about to get hit by this hurricane."

"Oh, dude, you don't even know what he looks like. Let me handle it. You just sit there and calm down."

We are silent for a moment. I'm pacing, trying to keep my mouth shut.

"What's the word around there?" he asks.

"Can't tell. Nothing on the news. Nothing really happening at the scene this morning."

"Christ, you went back? What the fuck were you thinking?"

"I wanted to know what was going on."

"You're lucky they didn't cuff you right there."

"Fuck you. There was a crowd. The cops didn't notice me." I get another beer out of the fridge.

"Fine," he finally says. "You lay low. You know you can't fuck this up. This is your last chance."

I swallow. I know. He—and Charles— have made it abundantly clear.

"I'll talk to you later. And, Jared," he laughs. "Don't gamble. You can't afford it."

"Fuck you." I don't say it out loud until after I hang up.

FOUR

I wait the rest of the afternoon for Joey to call back. I've got the TV and radio on, hoping to hear something about the theft. On the six o'clock local news, they re-run the same story from noon. Nothing new. No leads.

At least there is that.

Joey hasn't always been such a dick. We used to be friends. We met in college, watching a boxing match at a bar. Learned we both liked playing cards. Had a few good trips to Vegas. Then he started winning. I started losing. I borrowed money, thinking that the next bet would be the one that would finally pay off. He kept loaning me money, I kept gambling it away. He eventually moved out to Vegas; I stayed in Nashville, driving to Biloxi every few months. Occasionally I'd win, but it was never enough. Joey became well known on the professional poker circuit. I became a stupid cliché. Broke. Living on people's couches as long as they would let me stay, then moving on to another friend or relative. I had lots of guys on my ass; I owed everyone something.

And then Joey called. Out of the blue. Said he was in town, asked me to meet him at a bar down on Lower Broadway. The playoffs were on—March Madness—we played pool while we watched. We'd bet on opposing teams. It should have been easy money for me, North Carolina was the top seed. But Villanova wasn't letting up, and I was starting to worry about how I was going to cover my loss when Joey sat down and promised to make all my problems go away, including the thirty thousand I owed *him*.

He told me about this town in Northern Minnesota. "It's in the middle of fucking nowhere, dude," he said. "But Judy Garland was born there and they have this huge festival for her every year."

"Who is Judy Garland?"

"Wizard of Oz."

I tried to remember the movie.

"Haven't you ever seen it?"

I shrugged and took a drink of my beer while I surveyed the table. I took aim at the eleven, but the cue bounced off the five and pocketed the four.

"Follow the yellow brick road?" Joey said, rubbing blue chalk into the end of his stick. "Munchkinland?"

"Oh yeah!" I watched the three and the two go into opposite pockets simultaneously. He was about to win. Again. "Munchkinland!"

"That girl."

"What about her?"

"This town," he lined up his shot, tapping his stick lightly on the table. "Eight ball, corner pocket." He shot, the ball banked off the side and slid smoothly into the hole he had pointed at. He stood. "They have a festival to celebrate her every year. Mickey Rooney used to come. And the Munchkins. They might all be dead now, though."

"What's that have to do with me?" I wondered if he was going to pony up for another game. He was paying for all of it: the beers, the games, I didn't have any money.

Joey walked over to a table and sat down, still holding his pool stick. I leaned mine against the wall before following him. "They have this whole museum there dedicated to Judy Garland. And each summer they bring the real Ruby Slippers from the movie and put them on display."

"And?"

"And you're going to steal them."

"Why?"

"Because I've got someone who wants them." He motioned to the waitress for another round of drinks. "And because I'm going to pay you."

"How much?"

"Does it matter? You owe me, remember?"

I took a long drink of my beer, avoiding looking at him or at the game. "How much?" I asked.

"Eighty g's. But you owe me thirty, so you'll walk with fifty."

I jerked my head around to look at him. I thought he was kidding. But he was calmly watching the game, drinking his beer, not really watching my reaction. He wasn't fucking with me.

"For that kind of money, why doesn't your boy just try to buy them?"

"Because they aren't for sale. And even if they were, they'd cost a hell of a lot more than eighty. They're worth…I don't know… at least half a million."

I tried to look bored. I'd stolen things before; it was pretty much my main form of commerce those days. But nothing like this. "How big of a job is it?"

"What do you mean?"

"I mean, what am I up against? Alarms, security, guards with guns? What?"

"That's the best part! There's cameras and an alarm. Glass case. Nothing a face mask and a crowbar can't take care of."

"What's your angle?"

"What's that mean?"

"Why do you want me to do this? If it's as easy as you say, why don't you do it yourself? How do you know about the shoes anyway?" We had been friends, yeah, , but not good enough friends that Joey should be bringing this to me because I was just on his mind.

"Look, Jared, you need the money, right?"

I nodded. I couldn't argue with the truth, no matter how much I hated it.

"Charles isn't a very forgiving guy. With your fifty, you could at least tide him over, don't you think? I'm trying to help you out," he said.

"Well, I appreciate it. But I think I need to take care of this on my own."

"Just think about it. It's a once-in-a-lifetime opportunity." He stood and walked back to the table, inserted quarters and began to rack. "You break this time."

I took my position, lined up the cue with the one, and shot. The triangle of balls exploded, two solids and a stripe went into the pockets. "Solids," I said, and lined up another shot. I sunk two more, then missed. I watched as he pocketed four balls, then scratched. The heist sounded too good to be true, so it probably was. But the potential pay off was high enough that I was tempted.

"Here's what I don't understand. How do you even know about this? Do you sit around looking for steal-able Hollywood artifacts online?"

He laughed and sunk the ball he was aiming at. "No, man. I grew up near Grand Rapids. When I was a kid I used to go to the Judy Garland Festival with my family. It was happening when I was up there last summer and I went to check it out. Pretty much the same— fewer Munchkins, because, well, they're old and dying off. Anyway, I took my little sister; she still likes the movie. And we went to the museum." Somehow, he was already aiming at the eight ball again. He called his shot, took aim, and won the game. "I can't do this myself, because I'm too recognizable up there. There's so few people that everyone knows everyone else."

"Great. So I'm going to be recognizable as an outsider?"

"Nah- I figure there's two options." He began racking the balls again. "First: you move up there. Say you're enrolling in the community college, part-time. Get a job, make a life. You won't be a kid they've watched grow up, but you'll have a legit reason for being there. The other option," he grinned, and I braced myself for a much less thought-out option. "In and out. One night. Go in, get the shoes, get out of town."

I actually liked the second option the best. "I'm going to need more money," I said.

He nodded. He had been expecting a negotiation. "How much?"

"Half a million?" I took aim, all the balls bounced off the rail cushions and stayed out of the pockets.

He laughed. "You're fucking nuts. The highest I can go is one-twenty five." He lined up his shot, bounced the five off the rail and into the eight, which landed in the corner pocket. We turned to the TV and watched as a North Carolina player sank a free throw and won the game. It seemed things were finally turning around.

I winked at the waitress. "I'll take another; he's paying."

*****

When I agreed to the job, we decided I needed to be in town long enough to make a plan. I moved up at the beginning of the summer. I talked Joey into a stipend for living expenses and had gotten the part-time job as an on-call maintenance guy at a resort working for one of Joey's friends. There is a bar at the resort, pretty much the only place I've found to hang out.

I get sick of sitting around the apartment, waiting for news, and decide to go there. I can throw some darts, maybe play volleyball on the beach. Let off some steam. I have a little money left, enough for a few beers. Especially since I'm leaving soon.

The night is balmy, but there is a breeze blowing off the lake. This is why I like Jack's. There are bars inside and out, every night in the summer there is a huge bonfire and people playing volleyball. I get a beer and survey the landscape. I know about half the people outside, and I'm sure I would know more if I went inside. Regulars bellied up to the bar, just like I do when I'm bored.

"What's up?" Eric slaps my hand as he walks up and sits next to me on the brick retaining wall lining the golf course. "Good weekend?" Eric's family lives in town; they are rich enough that he spends his days playing golf and his nights drinking. He's in college somewhere, home for the summer. He is supposed to be working for his dad's landscaping company, but I don't know that he ever actually goes. I met him one day while I was trimming a tree on the golf course. He's a good kid. I like having him around.

I nod, "You?"

"Worked. Kelly coming?"

Kelly. My girlfriend. For now. She would be excited to know I have the Ruby Slippers. That girl is straight-up obsessed with *The Wizard of Oz*. She enters Dorothy look-a-like contests and has several pairs of replica Slippers. She actually made me watch the movie with her on one of our first dates. I thought I was one lucky son-of-a-bitch—I was going to have to watch it for research anyway, before I started scoping the museum. To watch it *and* get laid for watching it…

"Haven't heard from her," I say. "I think she's working. Sherrie?"

He nods, but says nothing. I can tell from the look on his face he doesn't want to talk about his girlfriend.

I take a long drink of my beer and watch the volleyball game in front of me, the girls in shorts way too short for the cool night. Bikini tops peek out under tanks, not providing the support a game like volleyball requires.

"Enjoying the view?" Kelly drops into place next to me on the wall, taking the beer out of my hand and helping herself to a long drink.

"It's better now." I kiss her and taste the cigarette she smoked in the car. I wipe my mouth on the back of my hand.

She picks up my vibe. "Stop it. It was a stressful night."

"Then start smoking something that doesn't taste like shit." I try to put my arm around her waist but she pulls away. "Sorry," I say. "Want to talk about it?"

"Nope."

"Mind if I get another beer?"

"As long as you get me one."

"Eric?"

"I'm good." He tilts his beer at me like a salute. "I'll take care of Kelly for you." He pulls her in to his chest and kisses her head. He's taunting me, but he and Kelly grew up together. Basically from the time they were born. Their parents are still neighbors. They've always been best friends. Never dated. No reason for me to be jealous. But since they both know I am, they play it up.

I smile, ball my hands into fists by my sides, watch as Kelly snuggles herself into Eric's side. *Walk away.* I try to remind myself why I'm with Kelly. If she wasn't so fucking hot...

And Eric's a good kid. A good friend. The kind that will come get you when you run out of gas money. He wouldn't do that to me, or to his girlfriend. They're serious. I wouldn't be surprised if they get married someday.

Kelly's like an addiction. But if it doesn't hurt, it's not bad, right? And I've kicked worse habits. When I leave here, we'll be over. I won't give a shit what she's doing then. There's no reason to get bent out of shape about it now.

Maybe when it's all said and done, and I'm long gone, I'll send her a picture of the shoes in my backpack. I won't sign it or anything, but she'll know.

The line around the outside bar is three-deep, so I go inside to survey the possibilities. The crowd around the bar is smaller, but it's louder up here. There is a DJ, and the main dining room is packed.

My phone buzzes in my pocket. Finally.

"Hey man, you got a minute?" Joey asks.

I can barely hear him over the noise in the bar.

"Hang on. Let me go outside." I nod at Jessie, the bartender, as I exit the front door.

In the parking lot, a truck pulls up, pulling a trailer with two jet skis, and Brad and Rick jump out. I wave at them, then walk the other direction. I wish there was some place I could go for privacy.

"Okay," I say, talking quietly, on the edge of the parking lot, my back to the building.

"Holy shit man! You did it. Congratulations." The words explode out of Joey. I picture him bouncing on the balls of his feet like he does whenever he's won big. It's like our conversation this afternoon didn't even happen.

"Yeah." *I did. Now I want to get paid.*

"The Senator is very happy. He's watching the news, and there's been no mention of it. At first he was worried the heist didn't happen. Then he looked up some local shit on the internet and found confirmation. No evidence! Way to go man!"

I smile.

"So— here's the plan. He wants to wait until this storm blows over. He's in New Orleans, you know. Then, we're flying down there with the shoes. He'll deliver the cash when he sees the shoes."

"That's not what I agreed to. I said I'd steal them. You said you'd sell them. You pay me, and you can do whatever you want with them. I'm not fucking flying with them! The longer they're with me—"

"Jared, Jared," Joey said in a fake-calming voice. "Let's not forget the situation here. I did this as a favor to you. I can't pay you until I'm paid. And I think it's safer, don't you, for you to hang on to the shoes? If we start passing them around…I just don't want us to get caught."

I clench my jaw and look for something to hit. Son of a bitch! But he is right. He is in charge. And I am sitting with the single most valuable piece of Hollywood history in my fucking apartment.

FIVE

We end up back at my place. Kelly would have ended up here anyway, but I'm not sure how Eric and Brad got there. Rick went… I'm not sure what happened to him. I'm not entirely sure how I got here either.

Kelly is asleep in my bed. The guys are playing Xbox, sitting on my couch, drinking my beer.

I want them to leave.

I'm stuck in the recliner. I'm too comfortable to move, but too uncomfortable to go to sleep. I'm sobering up and I want to be in my bed with Kelly, but I know I can't leave these guys alone. I shouldn't have let them come here in the first place. I can see, on the corner of the counter, my face mask and glasses. The crowbar is propped behind the couch. They haven't noticed yet, but they're idiots. As soon as I'm out of the room, they'll go snooping through my shit.

Eventually they get bored with the game and switch to cable. "You get Skinamax?" Brad asks, pulling out a cigarette.

"You can't smoke in here."

"What?"

"You can't smoke in here. Landlord's rules." I don't usually care about rules, but she made it very clear that if they smelled cigarette smoke in the units below, I would be gone.

"Whatever." He lights it and takes a long drag.

"Seriously, asshole. Put it out."

Brad stares me straight in the eyes and puts the cigarette out on the coffee table, burning a hole in the top.

I jump up, the end of the recliner crashing down. "What the fuck is your problem, man?"

Brad and I are standing toe to toe. Eric jumps up, between us.

"Calm down," he says. He pushes Brad toward the couch. "Stop being a dick." He turns to me. "The coffee table is shit anyway. He added artistic flair."

I don't move, but he sits down on the couch and picks up the remote like nothing happened. "So, Jared? Skinamax?"

"Nope."

"That sucks." He flips through the stations, doesn't find anything that holds his attention, and leaves it on a local channel while he goes in search of real liquor in the kitchen cabinets. There is news on, tracking the hurricane. It could hit any time now. Brad joins Eric in the kitchen. I can hear them opening and closing cupboards, but I don't want to help them raid my stash. I keep an eye on the face mask and work on coming up with an excuse while I try to listen to what they're saying about the storm on TV.

"And now, we're going to turn away from the storm for a minute for some News from the Northland. Early last night, in Grand Rapids…"

I sit up so fast the end of the recliner goes down on its own. Brad and Eric come out of the kitchen.

"… broke in to the Judy Garland Museum and stole the world-famous Ruby Slippers that Judy Garland wore in The Wizard of Oz. *The shoes, which some estimate are valued at over a million dollars, were on loan from famed Hollywood memorabilia collector Michael Shaw."*

They cut to a video feed of a completely normal looking guy. I expected an old, fat dude with white hair and a weird mustache, wearing a three piece suit. This guy is wearing a long-sleeved shirt, jeans, and looks like he's gotten even less sleep than I have. *"It's just tragic. I've been bringing the shoes to Grand Rapids for many years. I never thought something like this would ever happen there."*

"Although the police aren't commenting yet, sources say that both the security alarm and the museum cameras were mysteriously off, and there are currently no suspects."

I exhale for the first time. No suspects.

"Holy shit, dude! Someone actually did it!" Eric says.

I look at him.

"I always said it would be a fun job," Brad replied.

I swallow hard. My pride, my ego wants to tell them I did it. But I know that would be stupid. They wouldn't say anything, they're drunk. I shake my head. I'm drunk. I need to keep my mouth shut.

"I think Jared here did it," Brad says suddenly. "I mean, look at the evidence. A *face mask* on the counter in the middle of August. And a crowbar."

I open my mouth to protest, but he cuts me off.

"I know, I know, you're going to say you went on the ATV trails over the weekend and you haven't put everything away yet."

I laugh. Maybe I should tell him. His story is better than anything I could think up.

"Jared, can you come in here?" Kelly calls, her voice still half asleep, from the bedroom.

"Jared, can you come in here?" Eric mocks.

I look at the clock. 4:45am. I need sleep. I get up. "Guys, it's been real, but get the hell out."

They laugh.

"Jared! Oh my God. Jared!" Kelly is almost screaming now. All three of us run into the bedroom.

Kelly is standing at the end of the bed with my backpack at her feet. The zipper is open. From the door, I can just barely see the red glint of sequins.

Fuck.

Kelly is shaking. Eric and Brad push past me to where Kelly is bent over the backpack. She's standing in my Kid Rock T-shirt, her legs bare, her arms by her sides. Even in the baggy T-shirt I can tell she doesn't have a bra on.

I'm suddenly completely sober.

"Get out," I growl.

Kelly looks scared. She can't tell if I want her to leave too. Eric and Brad look like they don't care what I'm saying. I grab their shirts and pull them to the door.

"You didn't see anything."

"Did you—" Eric starts

"You," I poke Eric in the chest, and put my face right in front of his. Our noses almost touch. "You. Didn't. See. Anything."

Eric holds up his hands and takes a step back. "Dude, wait. Was it really you? Did you steal the shoes?"

"I don't know what you think you saw, but you certainly aren't blaming me for that. Get the fuck out."

Brad steps between us. "Dude, calm down. What's your deal? We were all having a good time—"

I don't like Brad much anyway. And he's still looking past me at Kelly. I shove him, hard. He stumbles into Eric. That gets his attention. "If you ever look at Kelly like that again," I poke him in the chest and back both of them toward the door, "I'll not only break your fucking nose, I'll blind you."

Brad stands up and starts to press toward me, but Eric grabs him and opens the door. "What are you on, man?" He shakes his head. "Brad, come on. He's out of his mind."

The door closes behind them and I lean on it for a moment, trying to catch my breath and calm down. I still have to deal with Kelly.

SIX

She's seen them; there's no way of denying it to her. The guys, maybe they're drunk enough I can convince them they didn't see what they thought they saw. But Kelly— she's too awake to convince it was all a dream. Fuck. Damage control. I'm praying she hasn't touched them when I walk back in the room.

She has.

One shoe is sitting on the bed; the other is cradled in her hands. She's turning it around and around, looking at it from every possible angle.

"Is it really them?" she asks when I close the bedroom door.

I make a split second decision and nod. A lie isn't going to help. She can be devious and vengeful. Deceit doesn't play well. But maybe if she feels like a partner in the crime…

"So….you did it?"

I nod again.

"Why? How?"

I shrug. "I needed the money."

"You're going to sell them?"

"They're already sold. Can you please put that down?"

She looks at the shoe in her hand and flinches, like she had forgotten it was there. "Sorry." She gently sets the shoe down. "Shit, I'm sorry—" she reaches for both shoes, moving like she's going to shove them back in the backpack.

"Just stop!" I'm more harsh than I mean to be, but a lot nicer than I could be. "Just. Stop."

She backs away, hands in the air. Two sequins are stuck to her fingers.

"I'll take care of it."

I've already got my gloves on again. I pick the shoes up and gently wrap them in a towel and slide them in the backpack.

"What should I do? I didn't ruin them, did I?"

I pick the sequins off her fingers and drop them on top of the shoes. "Why were you digging through my backpack?" I try to keep my voice calm. It's not working very well. I'm tired. And Kelly's not stupid. She knew exactly what she was doing.

"I was looking for cigarettes," Kelly says. She bats her eyelashes in a way that makes her look sweet. Innocent. Vulnerable. It usually works. It almost works

now. "I'm sorry, I know they're in there sometimes—"
I turn away, open the nightstand and throw a pack at
her. She's startled, but catches them. Her eyes narrow
and seem to get darker, just for a second. Then the big
round doe eyes are back.

"I'm sorry—"

"Don't. Just don't." I see more sequins, and felt,
stuck to Kelly's shirt and the bed. I squat down and try
to collect them, careful not to get any stuck to my jeans.
Brad and Eric have seen the shoes. Kelly has seen them.
I'm fucked.

"I've got to make a phone call," I say. "Can I have
some privacy, please?" She opens her mouth, but I get
up and grab her by the arm. I can feel her bicep and
bone under my fingertips. I know my nails are probably
leaving a mark. I try to breathe in and out through
my nose. I want to hit something. I escort her to the
bedroom door, push her through it, a little too hard,
and let it slam. I pull Joey's number up on my phone,
and my finger hovers over the call button. I can't do it.
What would I say? *Hey, so I decided to have some people
over, and my girlfriend found the shoes. By the way, there's a
few sequins missing. That's not a problem, right?*

No. I have to pretend it didn't happen. I place the
sequins in a little pile on the nightstand. Maybe I can
figure out where they came from and reattach them.
There's no way to get all of the tiny pieces of felt, so I
take the sheets off the bed, balling them into themselves
and shove them into a garbage bag. I'll burn them
tomorrow.

Kelly is sitting in my recliner, her knees pulled up to her chest and the T-shirt pulled down to her ankles.

"Give me the shirt."

"What?"

"Right now. Take it off. Give it to me. But carefully, in case there's any more sequins."

I throw another T-shirt on the couch, far enough away there is no possibility of her reaching it.

She stands up and stares me straight in the eyes while she peels the Kid Rock shirt over her head. I feel a smile playing at my lips, looking at her standing there in just her black lace panties. "This isn't a fucking strip tease," she says, but still twirls the shirt above her head before she throws it to me.

So much for keeping track of any sequins that might have been stuck to it.

Kelly reaches for the other shirt and I grab her arm. "No."

She turns her head, her hair falling over her face, draping down her shoulder and chest.

"You've got to wash off first. You've still got fuzz from the bottom of the shoes— "

"Are you fucking kidding me?

I should feel bad. I'm being an ass. But I don't care. "Go. Wash your hands and face. Take a shower, I don't care. Just make sure you get that stuff off of you, and don't get it all over the apartment."

She stands with her hands on her hips, making her waist look smaller and her boobs look bigger. I fight the temptation to reach out and touch her. Instead, I take the Kid Rock shirt, put it in the garbage bag and tie it shut.

She turns away, steps out of her underwear and walks naked down the hallway. The shower starts, but the bathroom door doesn't close.

In my room, I take the backpack and bury it all the way back in my closet, then completely cover it with clothes. I put shoes in front of the clothes pile and wish for more possessions to block the closet with.

I'm sitting on the end of the bed when Kelly walks in, naked, wet hair dripping little rivers down her shoulders, over her breasts, off her nipples.

"I didn't want to use a towel, just in case I had missed any of the fuzz," she says.

I nod. I know what she's doing, but it is still working. She walks over to me, straddles my legs. I rest my hands on her lower back, my fingers on the top of her ass. She's bent over me, her curved back keeping her breasts from smothering my face. Her wet hair is dripping on my pants.

"I'm sorry," she says.

"Good."

"Is everything okay?"

"No."

She bends down, kissing my ear. "Can I help?" She whispers, barely moving her lips.

"Probably not." My hands are roaming, pulling her into me.

"You really stole the Ruby Slippers?"

"Yes," I say as she moves her lips to mine.

"That's hot." She pulls away from me just long enough to see me roll my eyes. She laughs.

"Shut up." I pull her face back down to mine. She puts her knees on the bed, climbing on top of me, forcing me down on the bed, working the button and zipper on my pants, slipping her hands inside.

*****

I wake up when the sun comes in the window. We've only been asleep a few hours. I grab my boxers and pants from the floor and throw a blanket over my naked girlfriend. The way she's sleeping is going to kill her neck, but I don't want to wake her up. In the living room, I turn the TV on, waiting for the news. I need to know if they have any leads.

All of the stations are showing different versions of the same thing: either radar, a rain-covered traffic camera showing a big grey-brown blur of water, or some poor shmuck getting the shit kicked out of him by wind and rain while he holds onto a microphone with one hand and anything solid looking with the other. The announcers are saying things about buildings collapsing, people trapped, impeded rescue crews that can't get out. People who ignored evacuation orders are going to have to fend for themselves for a few days.

I sit, transfixed. I just can't wrap my hung-over, exhausted, mind around it. The sheer power of the storm…

I must have fallen asleep, because the next thing I know, Kelly is wrapped in the blanket, shaking me. "You have to wake up," she says. She has the remote in her hand and the TV is paused.

"What's up?"

She uses the DVR to rewind the news to just before the last commercial. They are showing the anchors in New York. "What?"

"Just watch the bottom of the screen."

In the black ticker at the bottom, random celebrity and other non-important news is scrolling. And then: *"A pair of Ruby Slippers, worn by Judy Garland in* The Wizard of Oz, *has been stolen from a museum in Grand Rapids, Michigan. Authorities are investigating but so far have no leads."*

Kelly mutes the TV and lets the commercials play. We stare at each other for a minute, and a smile spreads slowly across her face.

"I think you're pretty safe, if they're looking in Michigan." We burst into laughter together, but mine is fake. It's some stupid news station intern's fault. She either doesn't know MN stands for Minnesota, or she just assumes that, because Grand Rapids Michigan is bigger, the shoes must have come from there.

Kelly walks over to me and lets the blanket fall off her shoulders, revealing the curve of her breast. "Can I see them again?" she asks.

"I don't think it's a good idea. We shouldn't be handling them at all."

"Oh," she sticks out her bottom lip and lets the blanket fall further, barely covering her. "Isn't there anything I can do?"

"I just don't think—"

She drops the blanket all the way, takes my hand, and pulls me toward the bedroom.

When we finish, I sleep. I dream of yellow-brick roads and red shoes, but the dreams aren't bad. I hear movement in my closet. A zipper. I know what's happening. I fight to wake up, push up to sitting. Kelly's beautiful ass is bent over, her head in my closet.

"What are you—"

"Shhh," she turns around and holds a finger to her lips. My eyes linger on her breasts. She's so beautiful I forget what she must be doing for a minute, just watching her body.

I see one leg move, then the other, and all of a sudden she's just a little bit taller. That wakes me up. I bolt out of bed "What the hell are you doing?"

"Look, they fit!"

"Get the fucking shoes off right now,"

"Oh, come on," she tries to walk over to me, but the fabric is stiff and doesn't let her feet bend. She wobbles a little. "Don't you want to play?"

"No, I don't." I can see the shoes straining to contain her feet. They're way too small for her—they're practically a kid's size. "Take them off." My jaw is set and my fingers are balled into fists, gripping the sheets.

She sits on the bed and pouts, but pulls her legs up, one at a time, takes the shoes off, and sets them on the bed.

Great, gonna have to burn these sheets too.

"They don't even match," she says. "Look."

She is right. They're not drastically different. But one of the bows is slightly bigger, and they are shaped differently. One is narrower and more angular. The other looks like an actual bow-tie bow with large wings. The beads and sequins aren't even positioned the same.

"Flaws of hand-made?" I say. "They were made in like 1910."

She shrugs. "Really, they're kind of ugly. And I thought they were supposed to be jeweled? It's just plastic beads and sequins."

"Power of Technicolor," I mutter as I get up, put my gloves on, and carefully wrap the shoes again. They've lost a few more sequins; I add six to the growing pile on the nightstand. There is more felt on the sheets, but the bottom of the shoes were already worn, so I can't tell if any of the bare patches are new.

Kelly leans back on her elbows, pushing her chest forward, inviting me back to bed. I toss a blanket over her and go to the bathroom, taking the backpack with me.

"You don't trust me?"

I laugh. "Right. Miss Obsessed-with-the-Wizard-of-Oz. Of course I trust you. I've never seen you in the museum, drooling over these shoes. Just like I've never heard you talk about trying to steal them yourself. Just like you didn't already fucking put them on. Yeah, I'm sure they'd be perfectly safe with you."

"You're being an asshole," she said.

I pause for a second. She is probably right. But that isn't it. "No," I say, "I'm just trying to be smart."

I lock the bathroom door behind me and turn the shower on. As the steam begins to fill the room, I realize that the moisture might not be good for the shoes. Whatever glue they have holding them together is almost a hundred years old. I turn the hot down, make the water as tepid as I can stand, and shower as quickly as possible.

When I come out of the bathroom Kelly is dressed and at the door. "I've gotta work today," she says. "I'll call you later."

I watch her leave. That was too easy. She was too mad when I went in the bathroom to just let it go; that's not her style. I was ready for a screaming argument about how she could help me. I need to know what her angle is.

I need a better, safer hiding place. Kelly seems bent on fucking me over. I can't wait to get out of town and away from her. She knows what kind of trouble I would be in if I got caught. But she's getting some sort of rush from this.

I guess someone should be. I should be proud. I flip the TV back on and find the local news at noon. The FBI is now investigating the theft, but there are limited resources to devote with everything that is happening in New Orleans, and there are no clues.

There is no evidence. I did it right.

I just know too much.

I take the Slippers out to survey the damage. It really is minimal; I doubt anyone but the guy who really owns them would be able to tell. There were random sequins missing anyway, and the bottoms had been walked on during the movie. It's not like they were mint condition.

I consider separating the shoes, hiding one in my closet and one somewhere else, but decide that's more risky than Kelly coming over and finding them again. Instead, I put them back in the backpack, wrap that in a blanket, and put it in my one suitcase. I don't have a luggage lock, but I find a twist tie in a kitchen drawer and secure the zipper. Then I put the suitcase back in the closet where it was.

I need to do laundry. I can get a lock while I'm out.

I make sure both the knob and deadbolt are locked when I leave.

SEVEN

At the laundromat, all of the TVs are covering Hurricane Katrina. I check my cell phone; I've got reception. No calls. I consider calling Joey. I'm like a girl waiting for a date to show up. I don't even know where he is. What if he's with The Senator? He couldn't be. He would have told me. I try to remember what I know about The Senator while looking at the absolutely unbelievable pictures of the city I was in just a month ago. I don't recognize Bourbon Street. Besides the fact that there are no half-naked women or drunk frat boys on the sidewalk, all of the windows are boarded up. The wind and rain are still coming in sideways. The weatherman is huddled under the overhang of a balcony holding an ornate metal support rail. He looks like he hates his life.

I wonder how long he's going to hold on. How long I'm going to have to hold on.

They're talking about flooding. Whole neighborhoods being wiped out. Entire parishes under water. Anyone left in the city needs to try to get to the Superdome.

It's got to start getting better soon. It can't keep getting worse.

I check the phone, just in case. Still no call from Joey.

*****

My arms are loaded when I get home. Laundry basket, beer, and a bag from Wal-Mart containing several luggage locks (one for the suitcase, one for the backpack, extras, just in case), new sheets and blankets for my bed, and a padlock. In case I do find a better hiding place than my closet.

I unlock the knob, push the door open and drop everything on the counter. The beer goes in the fridge; I pile everything else in the laundry basket to take into the bedroom.

Something is wrong.

It's like when you have those side-by-side pictures that look identical, but really have a dozen differences.

I feel like I'm looking at the second picture and can't remember clearly what the first picture looked like. But something has changed.

But nothing comes to me. I must be paranoid.

I don't like how easy it is to get the suitcase out now that there aren't mountains of laundry blocking it in. Once it's locked, it's going to need to go somewhere else.

I open it. Too easily. I thought I had tied the ends of the zipper together somehow.

The backpack feels light.

I'm getting too used to handling the shoes. That's bad.

I open the bag and it takes a minute for my brain to register.

The towel is there. Grey terry cloth with six red sequins stuck to it. Fuck! They just keep coming off! I try to pick each sequin up and drop them in my pile.

I open the towel all the way, worried about the missing sequins. It's got to be getting noticeable.

But there are no shoes in the bag.

I rack my brain, but I'm so tired. I was going to move them; I must have done it, and forgotten. I look under the bed, under the chairs, pull out the couch. I open up the couch cushions and unfold the hide-away bed. It's fucking disgusting in there, but no shoes.

Step by step I try to go over what I did before I left, and what I've done since I got home.

I am sure I closed the suitcase.

I thought I locked the deadbolt too. It wasn't locked when I got home. What if I forgot? I've got to get some sleep. I'm getting sloppy.

But I *know* I put the shoes back in the backpack. Where else would I have put them?

The sequins aren't coming off the towel easily. I feel like if I can just take care of them, I'll remember what I did with the shoes. But the little fibers in the cloth are holding on to them like arms. Two bend. My hands are shaking. They're sweaty; it's getting harder to grip the tiny red metal. I lay the towel down and run my fingers across it like a rake, but that just bends more. I'm on the verge of completely loosing my shit when my phone buzzes.

No. Not now. I can't talk to Joey now.

It's Kelly.

Fuck that. I'm not going to talk to her.

I hit ignore at the same time I realize.

I call her back.

"You ignored my call," she says in her pouty voice. I can't believe I ever thought it was sexy.

"Where are they?"

"Where are what?"

I take a deep breath, clenching and unclenching my fist. "Where are you?"

"I'm in Duluth. I came over to see a movie at the IMAX."

"Who are you with?"

"I'm alone."

"Why did you go to the movies alone?"

"I thought you were mad at me. You were kind of a jerk this morning."

She's fucking with me. I can tell by the pitch of her voice. I have to make her feel better. Make her happy again. "I'm sorry. I was just tired this morning. I would have gone to the movies with you." It doesn't even bother me to lie to her.

"I am kind of lonely."

"Want to come over when you get back?"

"Can I spend the night?"

"Of course." She hates her roommate and spends most nights here. She never asks permission.

"What movie are you seeing?" I ask.

"Wizard of Oz."

"Are you fucking with me?"

"Oh, calm down. It's fine." She laughs and hangs up.

EIGHT

I pace around the apartment. I don't know what to do. I can't call anyone. I think about going to get her, but I would probably just end up passing her on the eighty miles of dark highway between here and Duluth. Plus, she can't know she's getting to me. She likes to get a rise out of people. She wants attention. Apparently I haven't been giving her enough.

Maybe she's not really wearing the shoes. Maybe she's just driving around with them.

Even if that's the case, I hope she is in Duluth instead of Grand Rapids. Everyone around here is talking about the shoes. At least in Duluth she has a chance of not getting caught.

Fuck it. I'm calling Joey. I need a timeline. I can't just sit here forever waiting.

"What's up Jared?"

"Heard from The Senator yet?"

"Haven't you seen the news, man? NOLA is destroyed."

"NOLA?"

"New Orleans. Geez. Get with the program."

"Fuck you. Have you heard from him?"

"Turn the news on."

"I've seen the news."

"Then you know that *New Orleans* is under water. Flooded. Gone. There's no electricity, no phone service, nothing. Half the people that stayed are probably dead. And the rest of them are fucked."

I take a deep breath and speak slowly, making sure my voice stays steady. "What should we do with the shoes?"

"I don't know, man." I hear him take a bite of food and get even more pissed off. He doesn't give a shit. He's so not worried about it, he's eating. "Sit on them and wait until we hear from The Senator I guess."

"And what if we don't?"

"I'm sure someone would buy them."

"Right. Just put them up on eBay? That wouldn't get me arrested or anything."

I can hear him chewing. I pray he's thinking up another plan. I should probably eat something. Maybe that would help with the shaking. And the headache. All I've had for the last two days is alcohol and adrenaline.

I try to remember how I got into this situation in the first place, and can't. It wasn't like I fell off the deep end, it was more like I waded into the pool and just kept walking even after I found out it was a wave pool and the water was too deep. Now I'm stuck. I can't get out of it. I owe money to Joey, but he's the least of my problems. And he's my only ally. Charles is going to call soon. I owe him a hell of a lot more than I owe Joey. He's more dangerous, and doesn't like me as much as Joey does. Did. Charles is not forgiving. And, I suspect, Joey owes someone money too. His share isn't going to buy a new house. Maybe a boat. But most likely it is going to pay off a dealer or a jockey. He likes the horses almost as much as he likes blow.

At least I draw the line somewhere. Marijuana, yes. Cocaine and heroin, no.

I do have some self-control.

"Well," Joey says finally, "I guess we could take them apart and sell the rubies. They've got to be worth something, right?"

I almost choke. And there is nothing in my mouth. "You're kidding, right?"

"No, I mean, it might take a little work, but I think the rubies could be split up and sold a hell of a lot easier than the whole shoes."

"Joey," I speak slowly, clenching and unclenching my fist, trying to calm myself down. "You're kidding right? You know that there are no real rubies on these shoes?"

"What do you mean?"

"They are movie props. There's no fucking rubies. There are sequins and glass beads."

"Are you sure there are no rubies? The beads are glass?"

"They might not be glass. They might be plastic. I don't know. I haven't touched them. But I do know for a fact they aren't rubies."

"Well, fuck."

I can still hear him eating, and, beyond his absolute stupidity, that is what pisses me off the most. "Listen," I say, trying to be calm. "Where are you? Why don't I just come to you and we'll figure this out together?"

"I guess—" now he's talking with his mouth full, and I have to listen to his teeth crunching then his tongue smacking around in his mouth while I wait for him to swallow, "–we have to wait for The Senator."

"Did you hear me? Where are you," I ask again.

"Maybe you should go to church and light a candle for him or something," Joey continues. "You're Catholic, right? I guess you better be fucking praying to God, Mary and whoever else that The Senator is still alive and has some money for us."

The line goes dead.

Fuck this. I can't hunt Joey down; he could be anywhere. I've got to get rid of the shoes before I get caught with them, though. I grab my laptop and start searching. I don't even know how to go about trying to sell these shoes, but someone besides The Senator must want them. At this point, I'm not even being greedy. I just want enough to get out of this whole situation safely.

I hear a key in the door and slam the laptop closed. Kelly bounces in, a tote bag slung over her shoulder. She is wearing a black skirt that barely covers her ass and a pink halter top. Her nipples are standing out like headlights. Even if they weren't, the shirt leaves little to the imagination. "Honey, I'm home!"

"Where are the fucking shoes?"

"Oh, these?" she swings the bag back and forth. "They're just fine. Are you in a better mood than this morning?"

I take a deep breath. I am going to have to get her on my side.

Or kill her.

I smile a little. I would never do it. I'm not violent. I'm just a normal criminal.

"Did you have fun?" I really don't care what she has to say, but she can't think I'm mad.

"I did. It was a quiet drive, kind of nice to do by myself. I was a little afraid I was going to get lost, I don't know if I've ever actually driven to Duluth alone before. And where the highway splits, I ended up in Proctor. But it was okay. I wanted to go down to Canal Park anyway, that's where I ended up. I'm just used to driving through Hermantown."

I nod, walk to the kitchen, and open the fridge. All that's in there is beer, mustard, and bologna that I can see is moldy even without picking up the package.

"Do you have any food at your place?" I ask.

"Probably not. Erin's boyfriend is staying with us, he eats pretty much everything he can find and never buys anything. I've been eating at work. You hungry?"

I nod. "Let's go to Country Kitchen," I say. I don't want to go out. But I'm starving. She'll think I'm not worried about the shoes if I don't mention them.

"Okay," she says, setting the bag on the couch. "Let me go freshen up."

I nod. As soon as the bathroom door closes I quickly and quietly take the shoes out and put them back in the suitcase waiting on the floor of the bedroom, lock it, and shove the key as far into my pocket as I can. I don't even check for damage. I don't trust myself to hold my temper any longer.

NINE

"Do you mind if I sleep at my place tonight?"
Kelly bats her eyelashes at me over the wood-
veneered table in our booth at Country Kitchen,
the only twenty-four-hour restaurant in Grand Rapids.
I'd rather have gone somewhere that served alcohol,
but most of those places are already closed. I thought
about suggesting Jack's, but was afraid Eric and Brad
might be there. I haven't decided how to deal with that
situation yet.

"Huh?" I'm wolfing down my fries so fast I had to
have heard her wrong. Two hours ago she asked to stay
with me. Nothing else's going right— why should I get
a night alone?

She looks a little disgusted as she watches me eat and waits until I pause before speaking again.

"You hungry?"

"I'm starving. You going to finish your sandwich?"

She passes her plate over to me. She hasn't eaten much at all, probably because she had popcorn at the movie. Maybe she went to dinner in Duluth. I purposefully haven't asked her about it because I'm not going to fight about it. That's what she wants, the fight. I'm not playing her game. She's going to play mine.

"I'm going to stay at my place tonight. Erin texted; they're going to visit her sister in Hibbing and stay up there tonight. I never get the house to myself." She pauses, takes a long drink, trying to judge my reaction. "I mean, if you want to come over you can—"

"I'm okay."

She looks offended and I backpedal. I need her happy. Or as happy as she gets. "I mean, I know how hard it is to have a roommate. I totally understand if you want to be alone."

Kelly flashes the smile that drew me to her in the first place and leans across the table, pushing her boobs together and almost out of her shirt. I wish she weren't so fucking hot. "Thanks. I'll come check on you in the morning."

I nod, taking another huge bite of her sandwich.

She gets up. "I'm going to take off from here, okay? You cool with paying since you ate all the food?"

"Of course," I wipe my mouth and smile. "But don't leave me here all alone. I'll be done in a minute. Sit down and stay with me." If she leaves first, she might go back to my apartment and take the shoes again. Maybe I'm being paranoid. Her smile is weird, off somehow, but she signals for the check and sits back down. I try to slow down, drag it out to annoy her, but I'm so hungry that I'm done and the bill is paid within five minutes.

She kisses me in the parking lot, pressing into me and letting her hands roam my chest, just enough to get me going before she bites her lip and pulls away. "Don't miss me too much tonight."

I watch her walk away, remembering all of the reasons we're still together, momentarily forgetting all of the reasons why we shouldn't be.

When I get home, I'm thinking more clearly. I take the Slippers out of the suitcase, put one in my backpack and the other back in the suitcase, then lock both. I've got to get them out of here, but I can't think of where to take them. I start researching the self-storage garages around town and surveying my apartment for something to store. It's not like I can go rent a unit and put just one suitcase and one backpack in it. I'm sure they watch for shit like that. Self-storage companies must do routine inspections for drugs, making sure people aren't renting spaces to cook meth or make bombs.

Self-storage isn't an option.

I have a beer, then switch to Jack and Coke. Six drinks later, I'm asleep.

"Hello?" The phone is in my hand and I'm talking, but I don't remember it ringing.

"Where's my fucking money?"

Even half asleep I recognize the growl. The voice, medium pitch but with an underlying gravel, haunts my dreams. I've seen what Charles does to people who don't pay him. He`s the reason I had to cut off contact with my parents.

I never should have gotten into business with him. I was stupid. And cocky. Sure I would be the one that paid him back with no problems. I just had to win.

Maybe I'm dreaming now. I'm certainly not winning.

"What's your problem? You can't hear?"

I remember what his gun looks like. I try to swallow but my throat is too dry.

"I said, 'where is my fucking money?'"

It's not a dream.

It takes two tries to clear my throat before any sound will come out. "I'll have it soon."

"You ain't trying to gamble with it, are you? Because I saw the news. I know you got the fucking shoes two days ago now. You should have the money by now."

Tell me about it. "The guy...he's in New Orleans, so it might be a few days—"

"You better figure something out, bro. You ain't got a few days. You feel me?"

I rub my eyes. "Yeah."

"I can't hear you, amigo. I said, you ain't got a few days."

I clear my voice. "I understand."

"If you and Joey think you can fuck me over, well, let's just say, you'll regret trying. But not for too long. Feel me?"

The line goes dead. What did he mean about Joey? Does Joey owe him too? Is Charles really somehow behind all of this? If we both owe him…if anything else goes wrong I'm completely fucked. Joey can blame it on me. It's all on me. I get up to pee, mix myself another drink, and wish I had some weed. Eric's always got weed.

Fuck it. If I don't go to jail I'm going to end up dead. I call him and invite him, and his stash, over.

TEN

When I wake up, the sun is streaming in the window and Eric is sprawled on the floor looking like he passed out while standing up. For a second I'm afraid maybe he's dead, but then he scratches his ear and rolls a little bit. I turn the TV on and find the news.

It's like I'm eighty-five years old. The weather and the news are all I watch.

New Orleans has gotten worse. A lot worse. The levee system around the city has failed. Everything is under water. And all the people they forced to go to the Superdome don't have food or running water. They're playing a recording of a lady on a cell phone.

"We're all going to die in here. They brought us here to die."

Newscaster: *"I'm sure they're doing everything—"*

"Like hell they are. They won't let us leave. The place is full of sh**. Actual, literal, sh**"

The beeping wakes Eric up. "What's going on?"

"Flooding in New Orleans."

He looks at me. "You okay? You got people there or something?"

"Something."

He looks like he wants to say something else, but I shush him as the TV switches back to the New York studio and the two anchors start reading the news.

"The tiny town of Grand Rapids, Minnesota, woke up to quite a shock on Sunday morning. For the last several years, the town, the birthplace of Judy Garland, had been the summer home of one of the original pairs of Ruby Slippers Garland wore in The Wizard of Oz. *Early Sunday morning, thieves broke into the Judy Garland Museum, smashed the glass display case, and took the shoes, leaving only a single sequin behind. While the museum has both security cameras and door alarms, neither was operational, leading authorities to question whether it was an inside job. Local police are accepting any and all tips and are waiting on investigative assistance from the FBI. However, with the situation in New Orleans, they're being told it could be weeks."*

"Wow, so the hurricane really is causing ripple effects all across the country."

"It is. In fact, we need to track that storm for just a moment. It has left the coast, but it's not losing power."

The radar graphic reminds me of a ninja star, spinning its way north through Mississippi toward Tennessee. They're talking about wind speed and storm velocity.

I realize Eric is staring at me.

"I need to make a phone call." I go in the bedroom and close the door.

My parents are still outside of Nashville, where I grew up. The first time I got arrested it was drugs. They gave me two options: get clean or get out. I got clean, mostly. I was doing okay for a while— graduated from high school, started at a community college. They even helped me pay for my own place, thinking the independence would be good for me. Like if they trusted me I would become trustworthy.

But then I started gambling. Card games at first, then college sports. It grew from there. I know it's my own fault. I made a choice. They tried to get a hold of me a few times over the years, every time thinking they were going to find a smart, well-adjusted kid who had just needed to get kicked on his ass to get his shit together. I could only disappoint them so many times before I stopped answering their calls and emails. Eventually, the calls stopped. Except Christmas. They would call me, together, on the speaker phone, and remind me that I could come home whenever I was ready.

I sit on the edge of the bed, my knees bouncing, staring at the phone. It's been so long. I don't know if they'll talk to me now— mostly clean, but still way fucked up. But I have to.

I dial, listen to the ringing.

"You have reached the Cannings," my dad's voice says.

"But we can't get to the phone now," Mom chimes in. "Leave us a message!"

I hang up. What could I say? *Hey, I see Katrina is bearing down on Nashville now, just wanted to make sure you're okay. Yeah, I can't come home yet. I'm working on it. But not yet.*

I've disappointed them enough. I don't need to add to it.

I take a few deep breaths. They'll be fine. I don't need to worry about them. Besides, I'm finally fixing everything. I'll get to see them again very soon.

I dial Joey and can tell I'm waking him up again when he answers the phone. "What the fuck, dude?" I say. "What's going on with Charles?"

"What?"

"He called last night," I say. "Said you better not be fucking him over. Do you owe him money too?"

"No!" Joey almost yells. He's way too defensive to be telling the truth. "He called me too," he continues, "to make sure I'm keeping you in line. That's one hundred percent your problem."

I don't believe him. But I can't make him tell me the truth, and I can't read anything in his voice. "I need to get rid of these things today," I say, "And get the fuck out of town. How long do you think it will take before the FBI figures something out?"

"Chill out, man. From what I'm hearing, you did a great job. No evidence."

"It's the fucking FBI!" I'm scream whispering, pacing around my room, praying Eric can't hear me. Even if he can, does it really matter? He saw the shoes. He already knows.

"Well, who did you think would be investigating? The fucking Grand Rapids PD? It's a high profile crime. It's probably a felony. Of course the FBI are going to get involved. You need to chill the fuck out or you're going to give yourself away."

"People already know!"

That makes Joey pause. Then he speaks slowly. "What do you mean, they already know?"

I run my hand through my hair, calculating how much I should tell him. I can't have him freaking out, but he needs to understand how serious this really is. "My girlfriend found them."

"What do you mean, your girlfriend found them?"

"I mean she was digging through my shit and she found the shoes."

"Did she tell anyone?"

"I don't think so."

"Can you trust her?"

I pause for long enough that he doesn't wait for an actual answer.

"What the fuck, man? She was digging through your shit? If you've got a crazy-ass bitch that digs through your shit then didn't you think that maybe you should have found a better place to hide the fucking shoes?"

I want to scream back at him but I don't.

"Does anyone else know?" Joey's voice is the same calm-cool I've heard right before he sucker punches someone who owes him money and isn't paying.

He's done it to me.

"I don't think so." I lie.

"What do you mean, you don't *think so?*"

I can tell by his tone I've got to be careful now. "No."

"Where are the shoes?"

"They're here."

"Are they secure?"

"They're locked up. But I'm looking for somewhere else, to get them out of here."

"You better get your shit together dude. If you fuck this up..."

I don't need him to finish the sentence. "I know." The line is silent, but I have to try. Wait!"

"What?" He is still there.

"Have you heard from The Senator yet?"

Joey laughs a little. "Of course not. Haven't you seen the fucking news?"

"Where are you?" I ask. "Maybe if I just bring them there—"

He hangs up.

ELEVEN

I go straight from my room into the bathroom, avoiding Eric completely. I had a plan. The plan was to get the shoes, get them to New Orleans, and get the fuck out of town. See my family for a few days. I didn't know where I was going to go after, but I was finally going to be free. No one would be chasing me, breathing down my neck for money I didn't have.

Now I'm stuck here, with the most famous shoes in the world, and no way to get rid of them. And I've still got people breathing down my neck for money I don't have.

The hot shower calms me.

When I go back to the living room Eric is sitting on the couch watching SportsCenter, and I've got an idea.

He looks up at me and I can tell he's trying to decide whether to say something or not. I get a Mountain Dew out of the fridge and throw him a Coke. I can feel his eyes on me as I sit.

"Do you still have them?" he finally asks.

I take a drink of my Dew and nod once. Eric grew up here. He's got family everywhere; both his sisters, his brother, his parents and his grandparents all live within a fifty mile radius. Someone has to have some place in their house where he could stash the shoes without being noticed. But it has to be his idea. I can't let him think I owe him anything.

His eyes get big; he didn't expect me to answer. He catches himself, regains his composure, and nods, like it's the most natural thing in the world.

"Are you worried?"

"A little." I hope I'm not going to regret this.

Eric looks like he's trying to figure out how to phrase his next question. I watch the TV. Finally, he leans forward, resting his elbows on his knees. "Dude."

I don't look at him, but I nod. He's processing it now, just like I did a few months ago when Joey hatched the plan.

"Dude," he leans back and takes a long swig of his Coke. "This has something to do with what's going on in New Orleans, right?"

"Yep."

"You in trouble?"

I shrug, trying to be nonchalant. "I don't know yet."

"Do you need help?"

I turn and stare him straight in the eyes. "Are you offering?"

"I mean, I want to keep you out of trouble. But—"

"But you want to make sure it will be worth your while?"

"No, no…I mean, that would be nice. But I can't…" he takes a deep breath. "Sherrie's pregnant. So I'm trying to figure that out."

"Woah."

"Yeah."

"So we're both up shit creek?"

He laughs. "You might be in worse shape than me. I'm just gonna have a kid. You… Someone helped you, right?"

I shake my head.

"Seriously?"

"Yep."

"But what about the security? No alarms, no camera? You must have had someone there that shut everything off for you?"

I shake my head.

Eric stares at me. "So, you are just the luckiest son of a bitch alive?"

"Felt that way for a minute."

"Now what?"

"The buyer is in New Orleans. Or he was, anyway. No one can get a hold of him. Kelly is obsessed with the shoes and probably going to get me caught. I've got to get them out of here. They weren't supposed to be here this long. I'm supposed to be long gone by now."

"What do you need?"

I don't let myself smile. But he's reacting exactly like I hoped he would. This is the most exciting offer he's had, probably ever. He's a good kid. He golfs with his dad. He just wants a little adventure in his life. And I'm not going to get him in trouble. This is just a very temporary solution until I can sell them. "Someplace safe to keep them," I say. "Any ideas?"

He nods, trying not to seem too eager. "Yeah, I can probably think of something."

We sit in silence for a while, watching but not watching the TV. I try to keep my legs from bouncing. I need to pretend to be in control, I don't want Eric to think I *need* his help. He *wants* to help. Because we're such good friends. And it's his opportunity to *do* something. The longer we're quiet, though, I start to worry. I need to know what he's thinking. What if he's trying to figure out a way to take the shoes for himself? I've got to get him talking.

"So, Sherrie's preggers, huh?"

"Yeah."

"Keeping it?"

He nods. "We haven't talked about anything else."

"What do you think?"

"I think we were stupid. But now we can't be stupid anymore." He gets up and finds my Jack Daniels, mixes it with his Coke and takes a long drink.

"You sure you want to get involved in this?"

"I already am. I'd rather help you out now than help the Feds when they show up."

I nod.

*****

I have to go back to work. The schedule has always been pretty loose— either I stop by to see if there is any work, or they call if something needs to be done right away. But I've been ignoring my boss's calls for the last week

Today he left me a message. "Either you come to work today or I stop calling you."

I call him back. "Hey, Andy. Sorry, I've been out of town."

"Bullshit. I saw you at the bar the other night."

Damn. "Yeah, sorry, it was a quick trip."

"I don't give a shit. You coming today?"

"Yeah, I can come in. What do you need?"

He gives me a quick rundown of the work that needs to be done. Decks that need to be repaired for Labor Day parties. A dock that got hit by a boat. A shed that needs to be built on the golf course.

"That should keep you busy for a few days," Andy says. Then he adds, "You okay?"

"Yeah. Why wouldn't I be okay?"

"I just heard…never mind. Glad you're alright."

"What did you hear?" My heart is beating so hard I feel like it's going to pound out of my chest. There's only been a few drugs that made me feel this bad, and I stopped taking them.

"Nothing. Rumors. You know how this town is."

I fake a laugh. "Yeah, I know. But I also know it's better to know what's being said. So help me out."

"Just stupid shit. That you stole the Ruby Slippers."

I'm glad we're on the phone and he can't see me. "Who said that?"

"No one. Someone said they saw Kelly with red high heels on. It was a joke. But then when I couldn't get a hold of you…" he laughs. "I didn't really think you could pull something like that off. Whoever did it had to be a professional. Or someone at the museum helped him. Either way, glad you're okay. Now get to work." He hangs up.

I clench and unclench my fist, pacing around the apartment. I'm going to fucking kill her. Even if it was just a joke. That's all it takes to get the cops looking. The TV is still on and I catch just a glimpse. They're still constantly monitoring the situation in New Orleans. And now there are reporters on the ground in Nashville. Hurricane force winds are battering the city. I put my fist through the drywall.

*****

I end up at Jack's again. The downside of working at the resort is that most of my money is spent here too. If only I could get them to give me a free room, I could get rid of my apartment. Then I'd have some leftover money.

I sit at the end of the bar, alone, watching the tourists trying to look like locals and locals trying to act like tourists. I've got a beer, but I really want a shot of tequila. I've got to wait for Jessie, the bartender, to get a little further into the night. She'll give me a free shot in a few hours. She likes to keep me at the bar, semi-sober, in case things get too rowdy. I'm not sure why, but people seem to listen to me around here. I don't look any different than any of them. Average height, average build, usually I've got a few days' worth of beard. Maybe it's that I've travelled. I've noticed the people up here don't travel much. At least, nowhere they have to fly. They go to the Twin Cities or up to Canada or the North Shore, but that seems to be about it. Even the closest major airport is over three hours away.

Tonight, everyone seems to be talking about the same thing: the fucking shoes. I try not to look interested while at the same time trying to filter individual voices to get clues. The best part about the small town is everyone knows everything.

A guy in a black button-down with his sleeves rolled up walks up to the bar and orders a drink, then goes to the jukebox in the corner and feeds it several dollar bills.

Shit.

It only takes a few seconds of the guitar riff at the beginning of *Welcome to the Jungle* for everyone in the bar to start bobbing their heads in unison. Soon everyone under the age of fifty is singing at the top of their lungs and swinging their drinks over their heads, saluting their high school football teams.

Jessie looks at me and rolls her eyes as *Sweet Home Alabama* comes on. She passes out the last drinks in her hands, looks around to make sure no one needs her, and comes to my corner. She leans on the bar in front of me, supporting herself on her elbow. Her brown hair is streaked with red and blond highlights and hangs straight to her chin. She's not much older than me, and, some nights, looks like she just got out of college. Other nights, though, like tonight, she looks like she needs to go take a nap for a few days.

"I guess I should congratulate you, huh?" she says.

I try not to let my expression change. "For what?"

"I heard. You don't have to lie; I'm not going to tell anyone."

"Tell anyone what?"

She stands up, raises her eyebrows, and tilts her head down to her shoes like she's looking over a pair of invisible glasses. "You don't want me to actually say it do you?"

"I don't know what you're talking about." I down the last of my beer. "I've gotta head out. Good to see you." I slide off the stool and walk as nonchalantly as possible out of the bar, through the lobby of the resort, and to my truck.

I've got to get a handle on this. How many people actually know?

Kelly.

Eric.

Brad, unless he was too drunk to remember. I need to see if I can find him, get a gauge.

Sherrie, Eric's girlfriend probably knows. Eric would have told her. But he would keep his mouth shut otherwise. So would she. They're good kids. They're about to have a baby. They need money, so they won't fuck it up.

So it all comes down to Kelly. And Brad. I don't trust either of them. Someone is talking, and it's just a matter of time before the information gets back to the cops. I've got to get rid of the shoes.

TWELVE

I call Joey. He doesn't answer. I leave a message, "I'm going to New Orleans to try to track down The Senator. Unless you want me to come to you so we can figure it out together." I know I sound desperate. I don't care. I am desperate. And this is as much his mess as it is mine.

He texts me back a few hours later. *Good luck with that.*

I don't have another suitcase, and I don't know what to do with the shoes yet, so I throw a few pairs of socks and underwear, a pair of jeans and two T-shirts into a garbage bag. I sweep the loose sequins into a cup. I'll figure out what to do with them later. I take that, the garbage bag, suitcase and backpack to my truck.

A few minutes later I'm heading east on Highway 2 toward Duluth. The airport there is expensive, but it's closer than driving to Minneapolis, and it's tiny. I might have a better chance of getting past security without them finding the shoes. I don't know how I'm going to do it, but I've got time in the truck to figure it out. I roll the window down and light a cigarette.

I realize about forty miles out of town I should have waited until the morning. There won't be any more flights tonight. But I have developed a plan for the shoes.

Usually I can get to Duluth in about an hour, but tonight I don't speed. I can't risk getting pulled over. It takes a full hour and a half. I pull into a Wal-Mart parking lot and shut the engine off. I know I shouldn't leave the shoes in the truck, but I can't exactly carry a backpack or suitcase into Wal-Mart or they'll think I'm trying to steal something.

The funny thing is, it's probably harder to steal something at a Wal-Mart full of crap than it was at a museum full of priceless Hollywood memorabilia.

I finally decide that putting both of the shoes in the backpack and carrying it with me is safer than leaving them in the truck. I don't like how much I've had to handle them. When I take the shoe out of the suitcase I notice more of the sequins have come off. I hope it's just the way the parking lot light is reflecting, but it looks like one of the big beads on the bow is loose too.

I've got to get rid of them.

It takes a moment for my eyes to adjust to the glaring florescent lights inside of Wal-Mart. The store is busier than I expected it to be at nearly midnight. It's the first lucky break I've had. With more people here, I'm less likely to be noticed.

I go to the ladies section. I don't know what I'm looking for, but I'm hoping something will jump out at me. All I need is something to make the shoes not look out of place in the X-ray machine. A dress, or a skirt or something. Other women's clothes. I can tell the TSA agent that I'm meeting my girlfriend in Chicago if he asks. Anything to keep him from wanting to open the bag.

I grab a black dress with a really low neckline— the kind that ties behind the girl's neck and makes her boobs look huge. I go to the underwear section and debate buying a pair of fishnets too. Kelly doesn't usually wear underwear, much less stockings, but I'm trying to remember what a normal girl would wear. It needs to look like a completely regular outfit when I go through security. I can't remember the last time I saw a woman in fishnets during the day, so I leave them.

I pay in cash when I check out. Back in the truck, I carefully line the suitcase with the dress I just bought, lay the shoes in and neatly fold my clothes on top. No liquids, no powders. I'll get some deodorant when I get to New Orleans. There is no reason for security to want to look in the bag.

I drive down the street to a Super 8. There is a bar at one end of the lot and I park toward the back. I'm hoping if anyone notices my truck, they'll just assume I had too much to drink and got a ride home. It's a risk, because I'm close enough to the airport now that people occasionally try to leave their cars here to avoid paying for airport parking. The cops tow those.

I pray the cops don't check until the morning.

I don't sleep well. I'm too busy trying to figure out how my life got so fucked up. I have a good family. Parents who did their best. They even took out loans to make sure I had the opportunity to go to college, even after I'd wasted half of high school strung out.

When I cut them out, it was to protect them. I didn't want assholes I owed money to think my family was a viable option for getting repaid. But it was also selfish. I couldn't take their disappointment.

I will see them again when I get back on my feet. When I sell the shoes, pay everyone back, and everything is okay again.

It'll work out. It has to.

When the sky starts to lighten I consider driving down by the lakeshore and watching the sun come up over the water. In my time in Grand Rapids I've only gotten to see Lake Superior once. Jessie and I drove over right after I started at the resort, before Kelly and I started dating. It was beautiful. Water stretching for as far as the eye could see, but somehow different from the ocean. Bluer, without that tint of green you can see under the surface of ocean water. We drove far enough north we could watch the sun set over a little cove, talking about nothing and everything. Then Jessie said she was going swimming, and, without waiting for me to answer, stripped down to her black bra and underwear. I pulled my shirt off over my head. We held hands while we ran into the water like little kids. The tiny pebbles in the bottom of the lake stung my feet and the water was freezing. But it was fun. How did I end up with Kelly? Kelly and I have never had *fun*, not like I had with Jessie. But Kelly was there, and very available. Jessie was just there...a good friend, but not throwing herself at me. Kelly was easy. At least, at the beginning. She was the path of least resistance.

Too often I've made decisions based on what was easiest at the time.

Not anymore. Something's got to change. This time, I'm running into the resistance. I'm running into the fucking hurricane.

I start the truck and drive the few miles north to the airport.

None of the ticket counters are open yet, but the departure boards are on. Everything going anywhere near New Orleans has been cancelled.

I pace and try not to look suspicious, but I'm too early. People are looking at me.

Lights finally turn on behind the Northwest Airlines counter and, even though I'm trying not to draw attention, I run.

"Can I help you?" A girl, probably a student at one of the colleges here, sets a makeup bag on the counter near her computer and looks at me with tired eyes. Her face is blotchy, her hair is still wet. She wasn't expecting any customers this early.

"I need to get to New Orleans," I say.

She narrows her eyes and shakes her head. "Sorry, that's not going to happen."

"Please," I lean over the counter, trying not to be rude but to show how desperate I am. "I *need* to get to New Orleans!"

She looks at her computer, types a few keys. "The closest I can get you is Memphis," she says.

"But...but..." I try to think of something to say that would make her feel sympathy for me.

"Do you have family there?"

"No," I say, too quickly. I realize I should have said yes. "But I have a friend. And I want to go help."

"They're not really letting anyone in right now. Not even driving. Unless you're with some big organization like The Red Cross or something."

"So, even if I flew to Memphis and tried to drive—"

"You would get there eventually, but I don't know how long."

I nod. "Thanks for your help."

"I'm sorry," she says, sincerely. "I hope your friend is okay."

"Me too."

*****

The drive back to Grand Rapids is long. I'm tired. And pissed. Of course I can't fly to New Orleans. I'm getting desperate, and it's making me stupid. I've got to get my shit together, or I'm going to be fucked. I have a couple of missed calls and voicemails from Kelly but I don't listen to them. When it's late enough, I call Eric.

"Dude, where are you? Jessie said you just bolted last night."

"Yeah, I'm on my way home from Duluth."

"Duluth? Why?"

"Long story."

"Did you take care of…"

"No. I thought I might be able to."

Eric is quiet for a minute. "Duluth might be a good idea."

"I was going to try to fly to New Orleans," I admit.

"Yeah, I don't think that's going to happen. From the news, it looks like a war zone down there. Have you talked to your guy?"

"No."

"What about whoever you were talking to yesterday?"

"He's no help."

"Well, I think I have an idea. But I still have to vet it. Sit tight. I'm doing what I can."

Eric hangs up right before my phone loses signal. Most of the drive is a big cellular dead spot. There's not much on the radio either. Country. I don't mind country, if I've had enough to drink.

My voicemail beeps as I start going through the little mining towns on the outskirts of Grand Rapids, letting me know my signal is back. I assume it's Kelly and ignore it.

Then I worry it's Charles.

That he's coming for me.

No. He knows I'm trying.

I avoid picking up the phone to look until I pull onto my street and see his truck, a brand new, jet black extended cab Silverado, parked in front of my building. He waves, letting me know he's seen me. I can't turn around. I can't drive past him. He'll follow me. I pick up the phone and listen to the message.

You better have a damn good story. And some cash. Because I'm coming over.

Fuck.

I slowly pull in to my reserved space.

Charles lets his truck idle slowly until he's behind my truck, blocking it in. There is no place to go unless I get out and run. But even if I cut through the woods behind the building I'll just end up on a residential street. He'll be on me within minutes. And he probably wants me to run. He likes knowing that people are scared.

I stand next to my truck, light a cigarette, and watch as he jumps out of his truck. It feels like a Wild West movie. He's even got cowboy boots on. No hat though, and he's wearing jeans and a t-shirt instead of a long leather jacket and chaps.

"Where you been?" he asks.

"Duluth," I say.

"You running?"

"No."

"What were you doing there?"

"Trying to get to New Orleans." There's no reason to lie. He's either going to kill me or not, there's not much I can say to change it.

"I thought you said you weren't running."

"I wasn't. I was trying to get to my buyer."

"He in New Orleans?"

"Yeah."

"You even know if he's alive?"

I don't answer.

Charles laughs. "Let me get this straight. You stole million dollar shoes, and now your buyer is dead. The shoes are too hot, so now you can't sell them anywhere else. And you still don't have my money?" He's in my face now. I take a step back but bump into my door.

He looks away, then I feel the crunch of his knuckles against my jaw and nose. There is warm blood running down my face along with the tears that spring to my eyes. I'm knocked off balance, but my truck holds me up while he punches me in the stomach. I fall forward, stumble, and hit the ground as his boot connects with the side of my head.

THIRTEEN

I drag myself up the stairs to my apartment door and lock it as fast as I can. I don't think anyone has seen me; if they did, they didn't offer to help. I want to push a chair in front of the door, but I know there is no point. If Charles comes back, and he wants in, he's going to get in.

I've got to get out. I've got to get rid of the shoes and get him his money.

I go to the bedroom and get the gun that is taped to the back of my headboard. I didn't think I would ever really need it, but now I take it into the bathroom with me. In the bathroom mirror I see that the side of my face is already swelling. I think my nose is broken. Both of my eyes are turning purple. I carefully peel off my shirt, flinching. I expect to see more bruising, but there is none. It feels like he cracked my ribs.

I step painfully into the shower, trying to wash my face without letting the water hit it. I refuse to think about the pain, even though the water feels like tiny nails being shot at my skin. I can only take shallow breaths and I can't raise my left arm very far without feeling a screwdriver in my ribs.

As I dry off, I hear a key in the door. I wrap the towel around my waist and hide in the hallway with the gun in my hand.

It can't be Charles. How would he have gotten a key?

"Hello?" Kelly finally pushes the door open and yells.

Fuck.

I silently go back into the bathroom and hide the gun under the sink. "In here," I say too quietly. I can't yell, there's too much pain in my chest. My jaw might be broken. It hurts to open my mouth very far.

"Hey—" she stops at the bathroom door. "What happened?" She doesn't step forward and try to touch it or comfort me or ask how I am.

"Nothing," I say. "What are you doing?"

She pulls back a little, acting offended. "What do you mean? I haven't seen you for a few days. So I came to see how you are."

"Who did you tell about the shoes?"

"What?" She puts her hand to her chest and her eyes and mouth are open wide, completely fake shock that I would accuse her.

"Who? Jessie knows. Did you tell her?"

"No, I didn't tell Jessie." Her voice is sarcastic, but I can't tell if she's really saying she didn't tell Jessie, or if Jessie is the only one she didn't tell.

"What the fuck is your problem? Are you trying to get me arrested? You know I could say you were my accomplice, right? You know that girl at the museum, I could say that the two of you—"

"Bullshit. You wouldn't. You're too proud. No clues, remember? You want credit for that shit." She pauses, cocks her head to the side. "How'd you do that anyway? You're not that smart."

Such a bitch! But what if she's right? What if I'm letting my pride—

"What the hell happened to your face, anyway?" she asks.

"I got into a fight."

"Yeah, I can see that. Did you get a punch in?"

"Fuck you."

I walk past her into the bedroom and start pulling on clothes. The movement sends pain so intense through my body and I can't tell what hurts. There are spots in front of my eyes. I have to steady myself against the wall.

"Come on," she says. "Lighten up. I was trying to make you smile."

"By making fun of me?"

"There are other ways to make you smile..." she trails her finger down my arm and lets her hand stop on the button of my jeans. "Do you need some cheering up?"

I pull away and wonder if she's blind. There's no way I could have sex right now.

"Are you mad at me?" She sits on the bed and sticks her bottom lip out, batting her eyelashes.

Something in me snaps. I'm done. "Of course I'm mad at you. You told— I can't believe—" I can't get the words out, between the anger and the pain and the panic that is rising in my chest. "I can't do this right now. I've got to figure something out."

"You need to rest. You're freaking out. Things will be better after you rest."

She gently pushes me down on to the bed. I try to sit up, but I can't bend at my waist; her arm across my shoulders is enough to keep me pinned.

"I'm tired too. Let's just lay here together, just for a little while." All of a sudden, she gets up. "Be right back."

I roll to my side and push myself to sitting on the edge of the bed. I have to stop, wait until I can breathe again, before I stand all the way up. I want to lie down, but I can't. I've got to figure something out.

She comes back with two little blue pills and a glass of water.

"What is this?"

"Advil. It'll help with the bruising and pain."

I throw the pills into my throat and drink the water. Anything to help with the pain. I walk out into the kitchen, pacing, trying to think. Kelly sits in the recliner, watching me. I thought I asked her to leave? Did I ask her to leave? I can't remember. My knees and arms are starting to relax. She comes over and grabs my hand.

"Lay down with me. Just for a few hours."

*****

I bolt straight up in bed and the pain knocks me back down. I can't breathe at all. My left eye is so swollen that I can't get it open all the way. It feels like I'm holding a wad of ice in my cheek. It's dark except for a light coming from the bathroom. I don't know why I woke up. I can't quite remember what day it is or when I went to sleep.

I reach to the other side of the bed. Empty.

I can't push myself back up this time, I have to roll onto my knees on the floor and pull myself to standing. I find a note in the kitchen.

Take two more of these and you'll sleep all night. I borrowed your truck. Be back later. Love you!

I go into the bathroom and look at my face. The eye sockets have turned a deep black-purple. I gently press two fingers into the green-purple bruise along my temple, where the toe of Charles's boot connected. My fingers go to my nose. It's definitely broken. It's not the first time, and it doesn't look much more crooked than it already was.

I wonder why Kelly took the truck. Probably needed gas in her car and she couldn't find my wallet.

I go back to my room and sit on the end of the bed. There is a path through the clothes on the floor, leading to the empty back of my closet.

Then I remember.

The shoes are still in the truck.

Kelly has the truck. *That fucking bitch.* Her phone goes straight to voicemail, all ten times I call it. I need to go looking for her, but I don't have a car. I could call Eric. He seems like my only friend right now. But I don't want to push him too hard. I can't owe him too much. I don't have anything to give.

I light a cigarette and pace. Fuck the landlord's rules. I'm not going to be here much longer, regardless of what happens with the shoes. I walk from my front door, past the kitchen and living room, down the short hall to the bedroom. And back. Eight steps. Over and over and over again. Trying to think of some sort of a plan that gets me out of this without going to jail or getting killed.

Maybe Charles will take the shoes and sell them himself. He would get a hell of a lot more money for the shoes than what I owe him.

But I know he won't.

That would make things too easy for me, too hard for him.

And if Joey owes him too— it's not worth his time. Or the potential damage to his reputation. He doesn't "forgive." Ever. It's cash or…

Maybe I should turn myself in. At least in jail, I would be safe.

I laugh at the thought.

I must be going crazy.

I call Eric, and he answers on the first ring.

"Man, I can't believe you did this. This is… I can't help you. This is just too fucking nuts. Are you kidding me?"

I didn't think it was possible, but I feel worse.

"What?"

"You gave Kelly the shoes? And an *outfit* to wear with them? What were you thinking?"

I sit down.

I think I'm going to puke.

The key to the suitcase lock was on the ring with my truck keys. She went through it. Of course. She's Kelly.

"Where are you?" I ask.

"We're at Jack's," Eric says. "Where the fuck are you?"

"I'm at home. She took my truck."

"You need to get over here pronto."

"I know. I don't have a car—"

"You're going to have to call a cab. There's no way I'm leaving—"

"No, I don't want you to leave. Watch her, alright? Watch the shoes."

"Yeah, man. But I'm not sure—"

"I'll figure it out."

FOURTEEN

"Jared Canning?" The officers are coming up the stairs when I step out my door.

I can't turn and run, so I let the door close and I stand on the *Welcome* rug the last tenants left at the apartment. "Yes?"

"That's quite a shiner, son. You okay?" One cop is about my dad's age. His partner is closer to my age. Both are clean shaven and are in surprisingly good shape.

I nod. "I'm fine."

"What happened?" The younger cop asks.

I shrug. "ATV accident."

He smiles. "It was a good weekend for it."

"Yeah." We stand in silence for a few seconds. I'm trying as hard as I can not to look nervous, but my palms are wet. "Was there something I can help you with? I was just on my way out."

"Where you headed? It's pretty late." Now the older cop is talking. They are standing uncomfortably close to me, blocking my ability to go anywhere. I shouldn't have closed my apartment door.

"Just over to Ruttger's. Jack's. Heard there's some people over there, thought I'd go check it out."

"Well, I'm Officer Cox," the older cop says, "and this is Officer Richards. We have some questions for you."

Cox is about the same height as me, but a little lighter with grey hair and wire-rimmed glasses. Richards is a big burly guy with one of those builds that can either make a guy solid muscle or complete blubber depending on whether or not he works out. Richards obviously lifts.

"About what?" I take an involuntary step backwards and run into my door.

"It would be best if we went down to the station. Can you come with us?"

"Am I being arrested?"

Officer Richards smiles a little bit, but Cox looks pissed. "Should we be arresting you?"

"I don't think so. What are we talking about?"

"Let's just go to the station," Richards says.

"My truck is gone," I said. "My girlfriend took it."

Don't panic. They don't know anything. There was no evidence, they can't prove anything.

"That's okay, we've got a car," Richards says. He grabs my arm and pulls me away from the door. Cox steps forward and Richards positions himself so I am stuck between the two of them.

I could argue. I know they can't force me to come in without a warrant or something, but I think pretending to cooperate might be a better idea. I can't do anything stupid.

At the station, the cops leave me in the tiny lobby and disappear down the hallway. There is a reception desk, but no one is sitting at it. There is coffee in the pot and a stack of Styrofoam cups next to it, along with powdered creamer and sugar. My head is pounding and whatever Kelly gave me is wearing off. I feel hung over. I consider ignoring the thin film that has formed on the top of the liquid and choking some down. Just for the caffeine jolt. I need something—

"Come with me," Cox sticks his head around the corner and interrupts my internal debate.

I take a step toward the coffee, but his eyes narrow slightly and I decide not to push him. There is no reason to get the cop pissed off right away. I follow him down a hallway, past a bunch of empty desks to a conference room. There are large windows that look out to where the desks and cubicles are, but no two-way mirrors or metal chairs or anything else like you see on *Law & Order*.

"Want a pop?" Richards asks as he sits down. He's got a Coke and a Pepsi in his hands and I feel like it's some sort of test to see which one I chose.

"Do you have Mountain Dew?" I ask.

Richards laughs. "Just a minute." He comes back with a can of Mountain Dew and slides it across the table to me, then takes the Coke from Cox.

"You still dating Kelly Morgan?" Richards asks.

"I guess," I say.

Richards laughs.

"What's that mean?" Cox says.

"I mean, we haven't broken up or anything. But we're not exactly skipping toward the aisle." I take a long drink and feel the carbonation bubble down my throat. I hope the sugar and caffeine hurry up.

"What do you know about the Judy Garland Museum?" Cox looks like he's going to be doing the majority of the questioning. He's leaning forward on the table. Richards is sitting back in his chair, a legal pad balanced on one knee. A pen is poised in his left hand.

I'm thankful for the swelling, because I don't have the best poker face. A big part of my gambling problem. When I try to control my reactions I usually end up making some weird or grotesque expression that completely tells whatever I am trying to hide. But when one eye is almost swollen shut, no one can read too much into what the other eye does. "Not much," I say. "I heard they had a big theft there recently. But I've never been." I don't know why I lied about never being there. What if they know I've gone as a tourist? I take a drink of my Mountain Dew and look away.

"Well, that theft is why we brought you here."

"I don't understand."

"We're hoping you can help us out."

"How?"

"Do you know anything about it?"

I shrug my shoulders. My hands are getting slick. I hold the can tightly in my right hand and keep my left on my thigh, under the table. I can't let them see. "Nope."

"Nothing at all?" Richards asks. There is something in his voice that gives me hope— he doesn't seem to think they were going to get anything useful from me. It's like he's being proven right.

"Nope."

"We know your truck was at The Sawmill that night," Cox says.

I go cold. I take another drink, trying to look like I don't know his point. I think about the drunk guy. There's no way he could ID me. Is there?

"We had a squad car there, around 1:30. You're truck was on his dash cam."

There was a squad car at The Sawmill right before I broke into the museum? How did I not know? There were no sirens. It must not have had its lights on, they would have reflected. From the back door of the museum I was completely blocked from view. I didn't think about how my view was blocked.

"You weren't staying there?" Richards's question interrupts my thoughts.

I shake my head.

"What time did you leave?" He seems like he's trying to hurry the questioning along.

"Around three-thirty or four, I think," I say.

"Did you see anything unusual?" He looks so hopeful I almost feel sorry for him.

"No," I say.

"What about Kelly?" Cox asks.

"What about her?"

"Was she with you?" Richards asks.

"She's kind of obsessed with the Ruby Slippers isn't she?" Cox adds.

I shrug. "I guess. I mean she goes to see them every year."

"We heard that she was spotted wearing some red, sparkly shoes in Duluth recently." Cox says.

It takes all of my strength not to tell them that they should go check out the bar at Ruttger's. I would love to pin this on her and be done with it, but if I do that, I lose the shoes and the ability to pay back Joey and Charles. Joey, I can deal with. Charles… "She's got a pair of red high-heels," I lie. "She calls them her 'Ruby Slippers.' I think she went and saw The Wizard of Oz last week, it wouldn't surprise me if she wore them."

"What do they look like?" asks Cox.

I hate the good-cop/bad-cop game. I probably have more practice at it than these guys. I just have to watch my temper.

"They're red. I think they have some shiny stuff on the sides or something. Glitter, maybe. I don't know. I don't really pay attention to her shoes."

"Yeah, I wouldn't either," Richards says with a laugh.

"Excuse me?"

"I'm just saying," Richards is sitting up now, and he elbows Cox. "With a body like that, I don't look at shoes either."

"Fuck you," I say under my breath.

"Excuse me?" Cox stands up.

I take a deep breath. He couldn't have heard me. He's not getting the information he wants out of me and he's pissed. I can't fuck this up. "I said 'Me too.'"

Cox nods once. "Here's the thing," he says. "You're not from here. You don't know how things work, so I'm going to help you out. You tell us what you know. You don't mouth off, and you certainly don't use any language. We're just having a discussion." He sits back down. "Now. You tell me. Do you think Kelly would want to steal the real Ruby Slippers?"

I think about how to answer. Kelly has the Slippers, so I don't want them to look into her too much. But I also want them to think that I'm helping them, so they'll get off my back. "Of course she does." They both sit forward. I can tell they're excited and I play on it. "Here's the thing about Kelly," I say. "I do think she has thought about wearing those shoes herself. She's probably even dreamed about it. But, honestly, she's not smart enough to pull off something like that."

"I agree," Richards says, nodding and writing something down. Without looking up he adds, "That's why we think someone helped her."

"I don't know who would have done that," I say, suddenly very nervous again. What is he implying?

"Listen," Richards is still talking but not looking up. "I know you've been around. We've looked into you a bit. You move a lot, don't you?"

I nod.

"Why is that?"

"Because I don't like being tied down," I say. I've got to get out of here.

"You've had some gambling problems, too, haven't you?"

I shrug. "I guess. If by problems you mean that I lose a lot and had to stop gambling."

"You lose a lot?"

I nod and offer as much of a grimace as my face will allow. "I tried to learn to count cards. I wasn't very good at it."

"We need to make sure he stays away from the casinos!" Richards says. Both cops laugh.

"You owe some people a lot of money, don't you?" Cox says, leaning forward again.

How do they know that? "We're working it out," I say.

"What's that mean?"

"I'm on a payment plan," I say. "Listen, I've really got to get going."

"How are you going to get home?" Cox asks with a smile.

I calculate my vulnerabilities. Leaving Kelly with the shoes, or possibly getting arrested. The "Advil" isn't making thinking easy, but it seems more important to do what I can to protect the shoes than worry about what will happen if they do actually try to arrest me.

"Well," I say, "Either you're going to call me a cab, give me a ride, or you're going to have to actually arrest me. And, since you don't have anything to arrest me for, I'm guessing we're going to choose one of the first two options." I hold my breath, hoping that my bluff isn't going to backfire. I don't know what they think they have. They have the truck at the scene. Close to it, anyway. They obviously think they know something about me, about Kelly. But they don't have much. They're fishing. I love that they think she's the motivation. It's just too perfect.

They exchange a look and Cox stands. "You're right," he says. "You've not been arrested, you can leave whenever you want."

"I'm ready to go now," I say.

"Ok. Hang tight and we'll get you a ride."

He's being too nice. Richards gets up and follows him out, and they leave me in the conference room, alone. I finish off my drink and wait. And wait. And wait. I look around, but I can't see a clock anywhere in the conference room, or in the office area. There are no outside windows, not that they would help anyway. It's nighttime. The dark doesn't change much.

Eventually, Richards comes to get me, sends me outside to wait for a cab. I don't have any cash, just credit cards, all nearing their limits. I've got to be careful. Maxing out on plane ticket would have been worth it if it meant finding The Senator, unloading the shoes and getting paid. But that's not happening. It's a nice night. I'm confident Charles won't come back, not yet. He wants the money more than he wants to hurt me. I hope.

I know it's going to suck, but I decide to walk.

FIFTEEN

I can't move very fast without hurting my ribs, so I'm barely halfway home before Officer Cox pulls up next to me. "Where you headed?"

"Home." I try to straighten up— I don't want him to see me limping.

He parks on the side of the road a little ahead of me, gets out of his car and leans on the side. "I thought you were getting a cab."

"It's a nice night; I decided to walk."

"Why didn't you call a friend?"

"Don't have my phone."

"Why not?"

I put my hands in my pockets and stop near his rear fender. "You guys kind of caught me off guard.

Had I had time to think about it, I would have probably remembered that I'd forgotten my phone with and gone back to get it."

"You seemed pretty nervous back there."

"Wouldn't you be nervous if the cops were questioning you about the biggest theft the town has ever seen?"

He laughs a little. "I guess so." He opens his car door. "You want a ride?"

"No thanks." I start walking again.

"I'll let you ride in front."

"No, it's a nice night. I'll walk."

He shrugs. "Suit yourself. But whoever did that to your face might be out here. Aren't you worried?"

I pause for a moment. Too long.

"That's what I thought. Your four-wheeler couldn't jump you, but whoever really did that could. We're going to figure this out, Jared."

I start walking again, pretending I didn't hear him.

"It's only a matter of time," he calls as he drives off.

*****

Eric is outside my building, leaning against my truck, drinking a beer. When I walk over to him I see that the suitcase and backpack are both in the seat next to him.

"Whoa. Kelly said you were beat up. But I didn't realize how bad."

I shrug.

"Where you been?"

"Cops." I say.

His eyes get wide. "They suspect you?"

I shrug. "I guess. It sounded a little more like they suspect me of helping Kelly, but it's all the same if they're looking into me. I've got to get rid of the shoes."

I want to punch the side of the truck, but I'm too tired, my hand is still bruised from punching the wall in my apartment, and I really just want to punch Kelly. I'm not an abusive boyfriend or anything, but sometimes I wish I could hit girls like I can hit guys. It's a stupid double standard. "Do you have them?"

Eric nods at the suitcase.

"Both?"

"Of course."

"Where is she?"

"I gave her a ride home. She was a little too tipsy to drive." He smiles and for just a second I feel a flash of jealousy. What else did he do with my girlfriend while I was with the cops? "Get in," he says. "We need to go back to Ruttger's and get my car. Then we need to get rid of these."

I nod. "Can I just go inside and get my phone?"

"Of course. You got any beer?"

"Yeah."

"Well, let's go then!" Eric tosses his empty can in the bed of the truck and follows me into the apartment. He goes for the fridge and I go to the bathroom.

When the door closes, it all hits me at once and I'm bent over the toilet, puking up what little I've eaten for the last several days. Every retch feels like someone is slicing my chest open with a knife. I definitely have a cracked rib or two. I hold my side and try to keep the tears stinging at the edge of my eyes from falling as I dry heave. Finally the spasms in my stomach stop.

I stand slowly, pain ripping from my armpit to my hip. I pull my shirt up, expecting to see the source of my pain, but, of course, there's nothing. Not even a bruise. I splash water on my face and brush my teeth.

"You okay in there?" Eric calls. I can hear him opening the fridge again. I hope he's sober enough to help me figure out what to do with the shoes.

"I'm fine," I say. I go into my room and find my phone lying on my bed, the display flashing.

Six missed calls.

All from Joey.

Well, serves him right. I've been calling him and he doesn't answer. Now it's his turn to worry.

I call him back without listening to the messages. I don't care what time it is. There's a better chance that he's up now than if I waited and tried to call him in the morning. "What's up?" I say.

"Where the hell you been, man? I've been trying to call you all night."

"Long story." No reason to tell him about the cops.

"Care to share?"

"Nope. You called?"

"Yeah. Well…we have a situation."

"What?"

"The Senator."

"You get a hold of him?"

"No."

"Then what's up?"

"I got confirmation…I mean, it's not one hundred percent, but it's pretty solid…" It isn't at all like Joey to be stumbling over his words like this. More than worried, he sounds scared.

"Spit it out, man. What's going on?"

He takes a deep breath and lets it out slowly. It's infuriating.

"Joey!"

"The Senator is dead."

All of the wind leaves me in one breath and I feel like I've been punched again. I stumble and fall on the floor next to the bed. "Shit," is all I can say.

He doesn't answer.

"But you don't know for sure?"

"No," he says. "But I do know for sure his house was destroyed. He lived in a place called Lakeview. The whole fucking neighborhood is under water. I don't know if anyone was rescued— they were all old rich white people. Smart enough to go to one of their other houses before the storm hit. God dammit, the Senator was a stubborn son of a bitch. He wouldn't have been one of those people standing on the roof of his house waiting for a helicopter. Besides," Joey pauses, "even if he was, he would have gotten washed off the roof before he got rescued."

"So he's dead?"

"Yeah," Joey says.

"Shit," I say again.

"Sorry, man," Joey says.

"Shit," I say. "I'm sorry, I know you were friends." I didn't even really know the guy.

"Yeah," Joey says. "Anyway, I just wanted to let you know—"

"Wait!"

I think he's hung up, but he answers. "What?"

"What am I supposed to do with the shoes?"

"I don't know, man. But Charles… He wants his money back. So you better figure out a way to sell them."

"He's coming after you too," I say.

"He doesn't know where I am," Joey says.

"Come on man," I hate how desperate I sound. "You got me into this. Help me out."

"Let's get one fucking thing straight," Joey's voice seethes through the phone. "You got yourself into this. It's your fucking problem. I was just trying to help out two friends. It's not my fault it all turned to shit. You better—"

I hang up before he can tell me what to do.

It's all on me now.

SIXTEEN

When I walk into the living room, Eric is sitting on the couch waiting for me, his beer long gone.

"You've got to leave," I say to him.

"What's going on?"

"You've got to get out of here," I say again. "I don't—"

"I can't. I drove your truck here. I need a ride to Ruttger's to get mine."

"I have to figure this out."

"I know. I've got an idea—"

"No!" I shout. "You have no fucking idea." I don't want to get him any more involved in this than he already is. I'm fucked. I don't need to ruin anyone else's life too.

Except maybe Kelly's. If it wasn't for her, flaunting the shoes everywhere and telling everyone, I could just put them in a fucking box and leave them on the museum doorstep.

Can't do that now. Her prints are all over them. My prints are all over them from picking them up and putting them away every time she took them out. The cops already suspect us. It's not like they're going to thank me for bringing them back.

I should have thrown them into Lake Superior when I was in Duluth. Maybe I should take them down to the river now, dump them, and run. Hope I can somehow lose Charles. And Joey. Be free. Sort of. I'd never see my parents again. And I'd always be looking over my shoulder. But I'd be away from here. Away from this. It's my only shot.

"Jared." Eric is standing in front of me. "You've got to pull your shit together, man. Calm down. I've got a plan."

"What?"

"Let's just go get my car."

*****

"So what happened with the cops?" Eric asks once we're on the highway, heading south out of town.

I fight the urge to look at the museum as I drive by. "Not much. They picked me up at the apartment."

"But they didn't arrest you?"

I shake my head.

"You went to the station with them?"

"I didn't want them to think I was hiding something."

"But they didn't hold you?"

"Nope. I told them I was leaving and they let me go."

He nods, looking out the passenger window. I can see his reflection in the windshield, illuminated by the stereo, but I can't turn my head. I'm grinding my jaw and I don't want him to see how scared I am. "They don't have enough evidence yet."

I wonder if I should tell him about the truck being in the lot. It couldn't help anything. But he should know what he's getting into. I shouldn't have asked for his help. Eric's a good kid. When I met him, he was golfing with his dad. It was my first day of work. We started talking and just hit it off. He's going into something big—engineering, I think— and he's got a future. I should have taken care of it myself.

We ride in silence for a little while.

"So what's the plan here anyway?" I ask. I'll hear him out, then let him down gently, with some lie that makes him feel like he was a help.

"Well," he turns to look at me. "My grandpa's got an abandoned iron mine on the edge of his property. My cousins and I used to play in it when we were kids. No one ever goes down there anymore, though. We can get one of those plastic boxes from Wal-Mart to protect the shoes, then put them down there. You and I will be the only ones who know, so you won't have to worry anymore."

It's a good plan. One that will get him thrown in jail if anyone ever finds out. One that, if I need to, I can use to deflect the cops from me. Tell them I think I know where the shoes are, pin it on Eric and Kelly. Eric's family could bail him out. And I don't care what happens to Kelly.

I'm ashamed at how quickly I flipped from wanting to protect him to being willing to sell him out. I wouldn't. I would make sure the cops knew it was all Kelly. She grew up with Eric, I'm sure she's been to his grandparents' house before. It would be believable.

"Why are you helping me?" I ask.

He shrugs. "You asked."

"You aren't worried about what's going to happen to you?"

"What could happen to me?"

I wait, let the silence fill the car. Finally, I ask, "Did you want to go out there tonight? Where's your Grandpa's place, anyway?"

"It's up by Chisholm," he says. "We better go during the day. If they're not home, it's fine, but if we're poking around on his property in the middle of the night Grandpa might accidentally shoot us."

I laugh. I love the people here. "Alright. I need to get some sleep anyway."

I pull into the resort and drive to the side of the lot in front of the lodge where Eric's car is parked. "Meet you tomorrow?" he says.

I nod. "Want to meet at the college? Eleven?"

"Sounds good."

SEVENTEEN

I sleep through three phone calls, and when I wake up it's almost ten a.m. It's the best sleep I've had in weeks, which is ironic because I wake up in a state of near panic. The Senator is dead. They've placed my truck at the scene. Charles is coming back at some point, probably soon, maybe today. I'm not as hopeless as I was last night, though. Eric's plan isn't terrible, and should buy me some time to find a new buyer. I've just got to get some money to give Charles. Something to hold him over.

I check my phone and see all of the calls were from Andy. Maybe I should go to work. I need money. But I won't get paid for another week. Damn two-week pay cycles. Doesn't matter. I haven't been going, so it's not going to be worth anything. I can call him. He might be able to front me the money. Anything to let Charles know I'm trying.

I sit with my feet hanging off the side of the bed and listen to the messages.

Where are you? I can't cover for you anymore.

Jared, you've got an hour to get in here.

Sorry man, I've got to find someone more reliable. See you around.

Shit. I guess asking for a loan isn't going to work now.

I think about calling Kelly, ending it for real, but I'm not in the mood to fight with her. I've got to get the shoes figured out— hidden, then sold, then gone— and then I can deal with her. Or not. I could just leave town and never talk to her again.

We've tried to break up a few times, but it's such a small town. We know all the same people, we hang out all the same places. We're like magnets. If we're anywhere near each other, we're on top of each other. Making each other happy and miserable is like a game to us.

I'm still thinking about her as I drive to the college to meet Eric. I'm tempted to take a detour through her neighborhood, see if she's home. The fact that she hasn't called tells me she's either still asleep, or she thinks I'm really pissed at her.

I am.

But I'm also freaking out, and, when she's not pissing me off, she knows how to calm me.

I stop at a light and look at the backpack holding the shoes in the seat beside me. I can't go to Kelly's. I've got to get rid of these shoes. Now. Before she has a chance to fuck with them again.

My phone rings and I answer it.

"You got my money yet?"

"Charles. Hi. How are you?" I try to keep my voice calm.

"You tell me."

I don't answer.

"You have any money for me?"

"Working on it."

"I'm losing my patience."

I fake a laugh, but pain stabs my ribs, making me cough, multiplying the pain. "I didn't know you had any to begin with."

"Oh, really?" Charles's voice changes to sweet and demure, like he can see me doubled over the steering wheel. "I thought I was showing you a great deal of patience. I'm sorry if you've misinterpreted it for something else. Kindness? Perhaps, generosity? Either way, I would think that you would be grateful. But you sound dissatisfied. Should we review the circumstances that have brought us here?"

"No." It's suicide to continue to provoke him. "I'm sorry. You're right. I am grateful." As grateful as I can be that Charles got me into his poker games, got me a hundred grand in debt, and hasn't killed me yet.

"That's what I thought. I'm going to give you until Sunday. We can go out for a drink and settle this as friends. Because we are friends first, right? Just like you and your friend Joey?"

*****

The drive to Chisholm is long and quiet in Eric's car. I watch as we drive through tiny town after tiny town, most with just a few houses close together and a sign announcing a population of a few dozen. In Hibbing we stop at Wal-Mart and buy a plastic shoe box and some food storage bags. Eric watches while I carefully slide each shoe into a bag, seal it, and place them side by side in the box. I wrap that in a garbage bag and seal it with duct tape then put the whole package into the backpack.

We drive through Chisholm, past all of the old buildings built during the boom of the mining era. Some of them house small, family run businesses, but most of them are empty. I wonder about the apartments above the street level shops. My apartment in Grand Rapids is above a shoe store, built probably around the same time as all of these buildings. I wonder if they are laid out like mine, and if the people who live in them are like me— temporary. Ready to go somewhere else. Stuck.

Eric follows a few turns out of town and soon we're on a burnt-orange colored dirt road. I can feel the car sliding slightly, the tires kicking rocks up and leaving a red cloud behind us. I hang on to the door as the car lurches over potholes and washboards. He slows down and turns onto an even rougher road— more of a trail, really— with grass growing on the hump between deep wheel ruts. Branches scrape the side of the car as we wind up a hill, and the sun gets blocked out almost completely for a moment before the trees stop abruptly and we are in a sunny clearing that is almost entirely covered with buildings. There is a converted trailer house, two normal sized garages, and one huge industrial sized building. Eric's looking at the house as he parks the car. "I think they're home. I'm going to go tell them hi. You better stay here—I don't want to freak them out."

I nod. The fewer people that can recognize me at this point, the better. But I do need to take a leak, so as soon as he's in the house I get out of the car and walk around to the back of one of the garages, near the trees.

"What are you doing?" The voice comes as soon as I start to go.

"Uh, sorry, just about done," I say, trying turn my head and locate the voice without getting piss on myself. I can hear footsteps echoing but I can't tell if they're coming from the trees or the garage.

"I said, what are you doing?" The voice is coming from almost directly behind me. Then I hear a snicker.

I finish up as quickly as I can, turning as I zip up.

Brad is nearly doubled over he's laughing so hard. "I got you!" he says

I try to laugh, looking toward the house and Eric. What the fuck? Why is Brad here? He's wearing a plaid flannel shirt that might have been brown and red at one time, with the sleeves rolled up to his elbows and the top few buttons undone. His pants, arms and face are covered with grease, as is his worn out Twins baseball cap.

"What are you two doing up here?" Brad asks, finally straightening up. "Holy shit, what happened to your face?"

"ATV accident," I mumble.

Brad nods. "Looks rough. So what are you doing up here?"

I don't know what Eric's telling his grandparents, and I can't think of any reason that we would be here besides the mineshaft. "We're on our way back to Grand Rapids," I say. "Eric wanted to stop over for a minute. What are you doing here?"

"I live here. Most of the time, anyway."

"What?"

"This is my grandparents' house. Oh—you didn't know? Yeah, Eric's my cousin."

"No, I didn't…" Fuck. Fuck. Fuck. Is Eric trying to screw me over? Does Brad know about the shoes? He was pretty drunk that night at the apartment, and he hasn't said anything about it since, but Eric…

We hear a screen door slam and look toward the house.

"Jared!" Eric calls. "Where are you?"

"Over here," I yell. Brad follows me over to the car.

"He was peeing in the bushes," Brad offers.

I shrug it off. "I had to take a piss."

"You could have come in the house," Eric says. He's agitated, and I can't tell if it's because I peed in the yard or if something happened in the house.

"Sorry."

"What are you doing here?" Eric asks Brad. There is none of the friendliness that I'm used to seeing between the two of them; instead, there's almost an animosity.

"Working on the car."

"Get a fucking job and stop mooching off them," Eric says.

"Fuck you," Brad answers and turns back toward the garage.

"Grab the bag," Eric says to me after Brad is out of ear shot.

"Are you sure this is such a good idea? Does Brad know what we're doing?"

"Brad doesn't know shit. If you want to do this, get the bag and let's get going."

"Are you sure—?"

"Yes. I'm sure. Let's go." He doesn't wait for me, just takes off toward the woods behind the house.

I consider his sudden attitude change, and my options. If I don't like where he's taking me, I don't have to leave the shoes. Even if Brad does know now, there has been a chance that he'd known all along, so I'm really not adding any more risk. And if this is as good a hiding place as Eric's made it sound, I don't have any better options. I reach in the car and grab the backpack. I have to jog to catch up.

"Hurry up," he says over his shoulder.

I'm already moving as fast as I can, but I try to speed up. The jog was a bad idea. I can't stand all the way up; the pain in my ribs is too much. I gasp for air and end up coughing, which hurts even more. I have to stop and hold on to tree branches for support. He eventually just slows the pace to accommodate.

Eric points to a creek in front of us. "There's no bridge. We're going to have to jump it, or wade through, or whatever."

I nod. The water is running fairly quickly and I can't see the bottom. I don't swim, and there is no way my ribs will let me make a five-foot jump. I'm less worried about me, though, than what would happen if I slipped and the shoes got wet. I consider the distance to the opposite bank and weigh what would be worse — the impact of me throwing the backpack across, or the chance of the shoes getting wet if I miss the jump.

"I'll go first, you can throw me the backpack, then you can jump," Eric says, reading my thoughts.

"No fucking way," I say.

"What's your problem?"

"Sorry, man," I say, "but how do I know you're not going to take off running and leave me out here to get lost?"

Eric looks honestly offended, and I feel bad for a split second. I remind myself he is a good kid. But it's still too big a risk.

He shrugs. "Whatever. The water looks pretty low. We might be able to cross more easily further down. Are you okay with walking a little ways?"

I nod. We walk downstream. The terrain shifts and becomes steeper. The creek is narrowing, but it's still too far to jump across, and the water is running faster, creating froth around rocks and fallen branches. The trees are becoming fewer and further apart, letting more sun reach us. I swipe my hand in front of me, trying to get the mosquitos away from my face.

"Let's just wade through it here," Eric says, starting down the side of the bank. "It's shallow; only your shoes will get wet."

I nod and follow him, trying to take small steps, but the bank is muddy and slick. I lose my footing on loose rocks. I try to grab at a tree to stop from falling, but my ankle twists the wrong way and I land, facedown, in the creek.

"Shit, man, you okay?" Eric says, jogging back to me. He looks like he's trying not to laugh.

I'm coughing and spitting out tiny little creek rocks as I push myself up, water and blood running out of my nose. The water is only about eight inches deep. I clean the mud and water off my hands, then reach around for the backpack. It's dry, thank God. But the movement sends stabbing pain through my ribs. Then I feel my ankle.

"That looked pretty nasty," Eric says.

"Yeah, it felt pretty nasty," I say, trying to move my foot. I cringe, and let out a low growl. I push myself backwards and crawl up the side of the creek bank. "Shit," I say through clenched teeth.

Eric is no longer smiling. "Dude, seriously, you okay?"

I shake my head. My jaw is set and I'm breathing through my teeth. "I think it's broken." I lean my head back. I want to scream. Instead, I take as deep a breath as I can and lean forward with my elbows on my knees. I hang my head down, letting the waves of pain-nausea wash through me. When they stop, I wipe my face with my sleeve and begin to tighten the laces on my sneaker to help keep the swelling down.

Eric has been watching quietly, and I can hear his nervousness when he talks. "Are you going to be okay?" he asks.

"Yeah." I spit. "How much further is it?"

Eric looks around. "It's not far, but it's not a super smooth walk either.

I stand and pain shoots into my foot, up my leg and explodes in front of my eyes in starbursts. Bile rises in my throat and I force it down. I put my foot back on the ground — I had reflexively picked it up and grabbed an overhead tree branch for balance — slowly shifting my weight until it is evenly distributed. I let go of the branch and take one test step forward, then another. The pain is becoming less, but I'm afraid it's because my body is going into shock.

"You sure you're going to make it?" Eric asks, holding his arm out like I might use him for support.

"Let's just get it over with," I say, ignoring the arm.

We turn away from the creek — I'm disoriented and no longer know what direction we're walking. I'm staring at the ground, watching for rocks or sticks that would cause me to lose balance. My ankle feels like rubber and I don't know how much longer it's going to support my weight, much less what it would do if it were tweaked. Eric has to stop and wait for me several times, even though it feels to me like we're practically running.

"Do you want to find a stick or something to use as a crutch?" he asks.

"No," I say. My teeth are gritted, I barely spit the words out. "It's fine. I just have to walk it off."

He looks like he's about to protest, but I walk past him. He gets the point and resumes leading. A moment later we leave the tree cover entirely and are on the edge of a small field surrounded by a barbed-wire fence with a *No Trespassing* sign. Eric holds the fence down with his foot and I step over it, supporting myself on the worn fence post. I can see past the grass where it looks like the earth falls away, and then rises up in a huge hill with newish growth on it. There is an old barn-like building with a long ramp coming off one side. On another side, there is a square tunnel that goes from the side of the building up in the air. At one time, it was probably how the iron ore was loaded on transports. The tunnel is supported by wooden trestles that don't look like they're going to last much longer.

"We're here," Eric says. "The entrance to the mine is on the opposite side." He keeps walking and I follow him, wincing with each limping step. We still have to hike out of here too.

The field is more precarious than the woods were; I can't see through the grass and am constantly slipping on the slightest change in soil. When we get to the edge of the mine we are able to get onto a relatively smooth access road that makes the final trek a little more bearable. I'm sweating and trying to keep my breathing under control even though I'm sucking air in and out between my gritted teeth. I'm putting less and less weight on my foot, even though I'm trying to force myself to walk as normally as possible. This would be the perfect time for Eric to take the shoes and just be gone— he can't know how bad I really am.

We duck under the tunnel and round the building. I can see that the door on the side is open, hanging by one hinge.

Eric pauses. "Someone's been here," he says, looking at the door.

Everything is covered in a thick layer of dust, and there are no foot prints or other signs of intrusion. "Are you sure?" I ask. "Couldn't it have just broken?"

We get closer and he examines the rusty hinges and the holes where they should have been attached to the rotted-wood door. "You might be right," he says. "It looks like the wind could have ripped it off. It hasn't latched in years."

I follow him through the doorway and we are at the top of a long metal staircase. It creaks and sways a little under our weight.

"Don't follow too close," he says. "It's not very stable."

I let him go the first few steps before I follow after him. I use the handrail— a piece of piping— for support as much as I dare, but it feels like if I lean on it too much it will break off. The concrete floor is about forty feet down. I don't think I would survive the fall. Having to shift weight completely on to my bad ankle each step is excruciating. He's at the bottom easily while I'm halfway up.

"Am I going to be able to find this place again?" I ask.

"Yeah, it'll be fine. I'll give you directions or something." He watches my hobble-hop down the steps. "Do you want me to just take—"

"No," I cut him off, ready for the question. I'm surprised it took him so long to ask. "I'm coming with. And I want you to talk through how we're getting wherever it is we're going as we go."

"Seriously, Jared, they'll be safe back here, but it's not like you'll never see them again. I can describe to you where I put them."

"No."

Eric shrugs and pulls a flashlight out of his pocket. "Suit yourself." I follow him down a tunnel big enough to drive a truck through and around a corner. "This mine shut down in the fifties," Eric says. "They were just starting to use bigger trucks in this part. I was thinking of taking the shoes part way down one of the smaller tunnels, where even if someone came in here looking around they probably wouldn't go."

"Okay," I nod and follow behind him. I hate every step. It's cold and wet and I don't know that the shoes are going to be safe here, but I do know that I'm going to be safer if they're here than I would be if they were in my apartment.

"Don't worry," Eric says, reading my mind again. "I've been stashing shit here for years. It's always fine. Just remember—the third tunnel on the left."

We turn off into a side tunnel and the passageway gets smaller and narrower, and, though I didn't think it was possible, darker. Eric walks confidently, instinctively knowing where to go. I keep a hand on the wall to steady me on the cracked concrete, concentrating on the glow of the light in front of Eric when he gets too far in front and I can no longer see his back. Finally, he slows down and starts sweeping the flashlight back and forth along the side of the wall, looking for something. "Here it is," he says, turning back to me. "This is my shelf." The glow of the flashlight reflects eerily on his face. His smile looks sinister. I squeeze my eyes shut. When I re-open them, he's reaching above his head, into small hole in the rock wall. He pulls down an old metal lunch box with a faded cartoon on the front, opens it, and shines the light on its contents. A GI Joe, a few other toys. He pulls out a joint and hands it to me. "This might help with that ankle," he says.

I accept it and reach for my lighter.

"NO!" Eric's shout echoes through the cave, coming back to us a thousand times. "You can't light it in here. You could blow us up."

"Bull shit. There isn't any gas in here."

"Maybe, maybe not. You really want to be the person to find out?"

I shove the roach and my lighter back into my pocket.

"Hand me the bag."

I give him the backpack. "They're wrapped good," he says. "They should be completely safe down here. It's wet, but it won't get through the plastic."

I nod. I want him to hurry up. Sweat is dripping down my face. I've got to get off my foot or I might pass out. And now that the weed is in my pocket...

He gently puts the backpack on the shelf, then pushes. It disappears and he slides the lunch box back into place in front of it. I have to flatten myself against the wall so Eric can step past, leading the way out of the tunnel.

"I brought you through the woods on the way here so we wouldn't see anyone," he says as we walk. "But there's a quicker way to get back, following the roads, if you want. With your foot."

"Is there much traffic?"

"Not much. And if anyone recognizes us we can say we were out scouting a deer stand."

"Maybe we could get a ride back."

"Maybe. It'd be a risk. Is it that bad?"

I nod even though he can't see me.

I can see the light coming in the door and Eric flips his flashlight off as we get closer to the steps. I'm concentrating on not thinking about the pain when a shadow crosses the doorway. I wonder how Eric got up the stairs so quietly and almost bump in to his back.

"What's going on in here?" I recognize Brad's voice. The metal staircase jangles and his body blocks out the light as he steps into the doorway.

"Hi Brad," Eric says.

"I said, *what is going on in here?*" He slowly starts down the stairs, letting each foot fall hard. The whole staircase sways under his weight and I can see cross-beams on the supports shaking. The loose bolts rattle. I wonder when the last time the stairs were reinforced. It's obviously been done since the fifties, or the whole thing would have fallen down by now. But it looks like it won't be around much longer. I wonder if it will make it through Brad's clomping. Each foot threatens to go straight through the metal mesh.

"Jared's never seen the inside of a mine before. City boy," Eric says.

"Yeah, I figured. What are you doing up here, anyway?" His words are thick, and his footsteps continue to flop, even after he steps off the bottom stair. He sneers at me, coming over to where I'm leaning against the wall. I can smell whiskey coming off of him, like all he's done since walking away from us is drink.

"I heard it was a nice place to live," I say. "Thought I'd check it out."

"What happened to your face?" The shadows sway with the wind, the tree branches outside of the door blocking and unblocking the sun in a halting, slow-motion strobe-light rhythm. I want to get out of here, but sprinting up the stairs and into the light is out of the question.

"ATV accident," I say again.

Brad abruptly turns away from me. "I don't think you should have brought him in here, Eric."

"Don't worry about it, Brad." Eric spits the words out. "You're not in charge. Grandpa knows we're in here."

"This ain't Grandpa's property, is it?"

I look from Eric to Brad and back to Eric. "What's he mean?"

"Shut up," Eric pushes Brad out of the way and starts up the stairs. "Who gives a shit? We played out here all the time as kids. Just because you think you're important—"

Brad jumps up the steps in surprisingly fluid movements. He moves onto the same riser as Eric and I can see that, even though Brad is a few inches shorter and probably thirty pounds lighter, Eric looks intimidated. He backs against the loose railing and Brad gets in his face. "I. Am. Important," Brad says. "And you better think twice before crossing me." He backs up half a step, his mouth open like he is going to say something else, but Eric turns and walks up the stairs.

"Well," Brad looks at me, "You coming?" He turns and follows Eric out into the sunshine.

I have no idea what just happened, or if I should be worried. I brace myself on each side of the railing and hop up the stairs, keeping as much weight as I think the rails will hold in my hands and off of my foot.

Brad has a four-wheeler outside the mine and we ride with him back to the house. Eric doesn't say anything about him on the way home. I can't form my thoughts into words to ask questions. He asks if I want to go to the hospital in Chisholm, but I have him take me back to Grand Rapids.

"Get as many pain meds as you can," Eric says when he drops me off at my truck. He'd offered to take me to the hospital, but I told him I'd be fine. The only good part about all of this is that it's my left ankle. I can still drive.

EIGHTEEN

I lie on the intake forms where they ask about drug use. I don't do drugs anymore, but I'm in pain and I need something stronger than Tylenol.

No one questions the story about the ATV accident when I explain my face. I use the deer stand story to explain the ankle, and it's also accepted. I have x-rays— it's broken—and they give me an IV of painkillers when the doctor sets it. He says we might need to discuss surgery after the swelling goes down.

"Have you ever taken Vicodin before?" he asks, scribbling on his prescription pad.

"No," I lie.

"It can be pretty strong. Start with one, you can take up to two if you need."

I look at the paper he hands me. "Thanks," I say. Two refills. But with his writing I can easily change the two to a five. I'll keep some for myself, but the money I get from the rest should be enough to tide Charles over. Show a good faith effort.

"Suzanne will be right back with crutches," the doctor says, holding the door open. "No matter how good you feel, you have to use them for at least four weeks. Longer if we do surgery." He is halfway out the door when he turns back. "Did you want me to look at your nose, too? I might be able to straighten that break—"

"No thanks. It's fine." It's started to heal. He'd have to re-break it. I don't care if my nose is a little crooked, but I know I can't handle much more pain.

He nods. "My number is on the prescription. Call my office today and schedule a follow-up for next week, please."

I nod, knowing I'll never call.

An hour later I've got three bottles lined up on my counter: Vicodin, Jack Daniels and Coke. I'm relaxed for the first time in weeks. When I fall asleep, I don't dream.

*****

Voices wake me up. They're muffled, and obviously trying to let me sleep, which I find funny. Especially when I realize one of the voices is Kelly's.

"He's awake," she whispers, coming over to me. She sits down on the arm of the recliner. "Hey, honey, how are you feeling?"

"Wonderful," I say and smile. It's true. The medication cocktail was strong, and its effects aren't wearing off. I wonder how long I've been asleep. I'm not even annoyed that Kelly is acting like a loving, sweet girlfriend. I let her lean over and kiss me, enjoying the view down the front of her shirt. I adjust and try to pull her on top of me, but she laughs and pulls away.

"We're not alone," she says, sitting up. The huge scoop neck of her shirt is pulled forward and her purple lace bra remains clearly visible. She's looking across the room, at whoever is sitting on the far side of the couch.

I can't see. I struggle to sit up more as Kelly moves back to the close end of the couch. I forget how heavy the air cast is and let the end of the recliner down, slamming my heel into the floor. Pain shoots through my body, cutting off my breath. I squeeze my eyes shut, waiting for the starbursts to stop. When I open them, Kelly has flipped on the side lamp and I can see that it's Eric sitting at the other end of the couch. He's got a glass of what I assume is Jack and Coke in one hand and my remote control in the other.

"You are alive," he says. His eyes look glassy, but that could be me, or the lighting.

"What time is it?" I ask. The streetlight is reflecting on the window, but I don't know how late it is. Or what day.

"It's about nine thirty," Eric says and stands up. "I just came over to make sure you were alright. Kelly seems to have everything covered. I'm going out. You mind if I take a few of these with me?" he asks, picking up the bottle of Vicodin and pouring the white pills into his hands.

Kelly jumps up and follows him. She still hasn't straightened her shirt. She must know she's hanging out. She's probably doing it on purpose.

"I want one too," she says, propping her elbows on the counter and leaning forward.

I stand, trying to ignore the waves of nausea coming over me. I know it's just the pills. And the booze. "I need more," I say and hobble over.

Eric has a weird grin on his face and his eyes are locked on Kelly's. I take the bottle out of his hand. "Shit, man, that's too much. I need these." There's only half a dozen left in bottle.

"I *need* them too," he says, popping one from his hand into his mouth like it's a peanut.

"You—" I hear the words in my head right before they come out and I cut myself off. Eric's as fucked up as I am.

He laughs, then downs the rest of his drink and leaves the glass of ice cubes on the counter. "Relax. It's just a little Vicodin. I'll be back tomorrow," he adds. "I've got a plan."

Kelly watches him leave, and I watch her.

"You want to fix your shirt now, since he's gone? Why didn't you just take it off for him?"

"What?" she looks down and pretends to be shocked. "Oh shit! I'm so embarrassed!"

She's not a good actress.

"You fucking him?" I ask.

"What?"

"You heard me." I pour Jack Daniels into a glass and follow it with Coke. Two of the pills come out of the bottle and I chase them with a large gulp, the alcohol and carbonation burning all the way down my throat. I know I've got to get straightened out and get back to the mine before Kelly does. I'm sure he's told her. But I've got to get past this pain first.

"I don't know what you're talking about," Kelly says, walking back into the living room. She turns on the overhead lights as she goes, casting everything in yellow-white light. She looks back at me with her big brown eyes and pouty lips and, instead of turning me on, it just pisses me off.

"You are, aren't you?" I say.

"Stop it," is all she says as she sits down and picks up the remote. "You're in pain. I don't know why you're mad at me."

"Are you fucking kidding?" I ask. "What the fuck were you thinking—"

"Oh, just chill out. Nothing bad happened—"

"How would you know? Were you here when the cops questioned me?"

That makes her look up. "What?"

"The cops. They were nice enough to give me a ride to the station since I had loaned a friend my truck."

"What happened? Do they suspect you?" She seems genuinely concerned.

I decide to tell her the truth. See if it scares her. "They suspect I helped you."

Her eyes get wide. "Bullshit."

I shrug. "They heard you've been talking. And they knew you weren't smart enough to do it yourself."

"Fuck you."

I shrug. "Does Sherrie know about you two?"

"Jared, shut up. You sound like a jealous idiot. Eric and I have been friends since second grade."

"What about the pills? Does she know he's an addict? He sure hid it well. Until I had something he could score I had no idea." I take a long drink and stare at her until she looks away.

"If you're going to be a dick, I'm going to leave."

I don't take my eyes off the television while I consider whether or not I want her to stay. I'm in pain and I don't want to be alone. "You can stay," I say finally, still not looking at her.

She lets out a "humph" and I can tell she's pouting, but I ignore it. After a while she gets up to go to the bathroom, then goes to the kitchen. She comes back with two Jack and Cokes and hands one to me. "How you doing? Do you need anything?"

I shake my head.

She sits on the edge of the chair again. "What really happened with the cops?" Her voice is gentle and quiet, the same one she uses in bed when she wants to talk and I want to go to sleep.

"They asked a bunch of questions."

"Do you think they'll catch you?"

I shrug. "I'm not sure." I look her straight in the eyes. "I wasn't shitting you. They think you did it, but that you had help."

She pulls her head back, like she needs to get a better look at me, and her eyes search mine. I don't blink. I want her to know that I'm not kidding.

"Where are the shoes now?" she asks.

"Are you serious?" I laugh. The pain in my ribs has been dulled by the Vicodin, too. Finally, for the first time, something is actually going right. He might be fucking my girlfriend, but Eric didn't tell her about helping me hide the shoes. I laugh again. I almost don't mind that he took all my Vicodin.

She pouts. "But what if they question me? What am I supposed to say?"

"You will tell them you have no idea where the shoes are, because that's the truth. And when they ask about the ones you claimed to be wearing the last few days..." I wait for her to finish the thought for me.

She looks scared. "I don't know," she says.

"You will fucking lie," I say, staring at her. I wish I could stand up, grab her by the shoulders, and shake some sense in to her. I want to scare her. A lot. Enough that she stops being so stupid.

NINETEEN

Eric shows up around noon with coffee in one hand and a notebook in the other. "Thought you might need some of this today." He hands me the coffee and throws the notebook on the table.

The Vicodin bottle is empty and I'm in pain. "What's your plan?" I snap. "And where are my pills?" I'm sitting on the couch, my foot propped up on the crappy coffee table, watching the news. It's still near-constant coverage of Hurricane Katrina, but I've seen mentions of the theft on several national news shows. Mostly just asking for anyone with information to come forward, which makes me feel a little better.

"Where's Kelly?" he asks.

"Why do you want to know?"

Eric shrugs. "I just didn't know if you wanted her to be a part of this plan or not."

I sip the coffee and look at him. "You think it would be a good idea to have her a part of it?"

He shrugs again.

"Let me ask you something," I say. "You think Kelly's..." I fake hesitation. "I'm thinking about breaking up with her."

He raises his eyebrows and I see it in his eyes— just a flash, but it's there. Excitement. "Why?" he asks.

"All this with the shoes," I lie. "She just seems to be a liability here."

"You're probably right," he says.

I nod. Anyone who knows Kelly would know that breaking up with her would be the stupidest possible move for me. When she's angry and jealous, she's even more dangerous than normal. She loves revenge. I'd save myself time by just going to the cops rather than breaking up with her. Which means now I can't trust Eric either, because he's more interested in fucking my girlfriend than getting me through this.

What if he's only pretending to help at all? Maybe this is all just a plan to get me caught so they can be together.

"Let's hear it," I say. "What's your plan?"

"You need money, right? You don't care about the actual shoes?"

"Right."

"Write a ransom letter. How much do you need? Half a million?"

"Quarter, actually."

"Alright, then, even better. Quarter of a million. Easy. The shoes must be insured for at least half, maybe more. Get the money, give back the shoes, and get out of town before you get caught. Everyone is happy."

It's a great idea. If we can figure out a way to do the exchange without getting caught...this could all be over in the next few days. No trying to figure out how to sell them, no negotiating with Charles for more time. Selling them is the only other option and I can't even figure out where to start.

"Okay," I say. "I like the idea. But how does it work?"

He shrugs. He's pouring himself a Jack and Coke. I don't know why I never noticed before how much he drinks. "I thought you might have some ideas."

"And you want a cut?"

He shrugs again and doesn't look at me. "Whatever you think is fair, buddy."

"I'll tell you what," I say. I stand, but it takes a minute and diminishes any amount of intimidation I thought I might have been able to muster. "You get me more Vicodin, and we can talk about cutting you in. Otherwise," I hobble to the kitchen counter, "I think we should just count that as your payment. And," I take the glass from his hand and take a long drink, "stop drinking all my booze."

He looks at me for a minute. A smile slowly spreads across his face and he laughs. "Okay, man, whatever." He gets another glass and makes himself a new drink. "You ever written a ransom note before?"

"Of course not. Have you?"

"Once, when I was a kid, I tried to hold my sister for ransom."

"Yeah? How'd that go for you?"

"Not well. I was hoping to double my allowance. Instead, I lost it. Got the shit kicked out of me too."

"I'd imagine."

I wait for him to continue with his plan, but he just looks at me. I realize that was the extent of his thought process. "I guess we need to figure out how to do it without it being traced back to us. In the movies they either use typewriters, or they cut the letters out of magazines and glue them onto a piece of paper."

"I don't have the patience for glue."

"Yeah, me neither," I say. "But the typewriter could work."

"Why don't you just use your computer?"

"I don't have a printer."

"Isn't there one at Ruttger's you could use?"

"I'll figure something out," I say. I need to separate myself from him. Let him think that everything is okay, I can't deal with him getting mad, but I can't have him be any more a part of this. "Do we need to do something about Brad?"

"What do you mean?"

"We going to be okay?"

Eric nods, but doesn't meet my eyes. "He doesn't know about my tunnel. But he thinks he's the overseer and protector of the mine. He's a *Rescue Volunteer*. Meaning, he has no power, but he thinks he's important."

"But you don't think he'll go snooping around?"

Eric shakes his head. "Even if he does, he won't find anything."

*****

After Eric's gone, I sit down at the table with my computer and search "Ransom Letter" on the internet. The results are surprising. Most are for ransom letter generators. They take the text that you give them and turn them into what looks like cut out letters. It takes me a while to find any information on what I should actually put into the letter, and even then it's mostly old ransom letters from kidnappings.

From what I can tell, both the victim and the kidnapper usually ended up dead.

I finally settle for short and sweet. *I have the Ruby Slippers.* Then, I'm stuck. How do I get the money? How do they get in contact with me? I can't exactly give them my number and say *Please call.*

I think back to the movie kidnappings I've seen and add: *They are safe and in good condition. I will return them in exchange for $500,000. I will call the museum on Monday at 1:00 to arrange for the exchange.*

I save the letter to a disc and hobble out to the truck.

On the drive to Ruttger's, I try to think of a story to tell Andy to get him to let me use his computer, but decide to just straight up ask. He won't look at what I print. It'll be okay. Plus, I can probably grab an envelope and a stamp from him too.

The police tape is still in front of the museum when I drive by, but there doesn't seem to be anyone around. The billboard out front, the one advertising that the shoes are inside, has a hand-lettered sign slapped across it that says: HELP US FIND THE SLIPPERS!

I turn the radio up, light a cigarette, and try to ignore the churning in my stomach. I haven't eaten, I drank too much, and I'm in pain. That's all that it is. And I need to get some money. Now.

Andy comes out of the golf shop and meets me at my truck. "Sorry," he says, "Only current employees can pick up paychecks. The rest have already been mailed."

I'd totally forgotten about payday. But now I want my check. I grit my teeth. I can't fight with him. I need to get into the office. "Look, Andy, I'm sorry about how things worked out. I am. But I really need money." I shove my door open. The crutches go out first and I slowly lower my body down, trying to keep as much weight as possible off the leg. I hold my arms out, asking him to look at me. I know I look like shit. He's got to have a little bit of sympathy. "Can we at least see whether or not the mail has gone out yet? If it's here, can't you just give me the check?"

Andy swipes at a mosquito buzzing around his face and scratches the back of his neck where I can see perspiration beading up.

"What happened to your leg?" he asks.

"I fell. In the woods."

He nods and scratches his jaw. "And your face?"

"ATV accident."

I can tell by his eyes he doesn't believe me.

"You gambling?" He ran a background check before giving me the job. I assured him it was no longer a problem and he agreed to give me a chance. It was more than most people had done for me.

I look him in the eyes. "No. I haven't been gambling."

He just stares at me, and I look down, trying to look as desperate as I feel.

"Oh, alright," he says. "You want to wait here? I can go see if I can find it."

"No!" I say, too quickly. "I mean, I need to practice on these things anyway. And it's too hot to hang out in the parking lot."

He grunts and starts to walk. I follow as quickly as I can, which isn't very fast. He's through the maze of golf carts, lawn mowers and tools and in the office before I even enter the garage.

"I don't think it's here," he calls. "But let me go check the lodge." He walks past me and I see pity in his eyes. "Why don't you just wait in the office?"

I nod and wipe my sweaty palms on my jeans, trying to get a better grip on my crutches. I pick my way through the garage and into Andy's office, hoping against hope there will be *something* I can use to send the ransom letter. Anything.

I fall into the folding chair inside his office door and allow myself only a moment to catch my breath. I hook my crutch into his wheeled chair and transfer myself to it, then use my good leg to push myself back to his desk. The top is pretty clean, the computer monitor and keyboard take up most of the space. There is a basket where Andy keeps the invoices and bills he needs to take care of.

I shove the disk in and, while I'm waiting for the computer to read it, start looking for envelopes. In the desk drawers are pens and golf pencils, a few score cards, a few blank timecards. The file cabinets behind me are all locked.

The computer finally opens the disk; I double click on the letter, and hit print. I can hear the printer out by the main golf desk heating up. I grab my crutches, eject the disk, and hobble out to the printer. There is a large box of cards on the counter with a picture of the resort and *Thank You* calligraphied on the front.

Invitations to the annual membership thank you dinner.

I dig down in the side of the box and find envelopes under the cards, and a roll of stamps at the bottom of the box. I stick one on the front of a small envelope. I'm just starting to fold the ransom letter to fit when I hear Andy walking back through the garage. I force everything into my pocket and can feel it bulging. I sit down quickly, hoping it flattens out before I stand up again.

"You better appreciate this," he says. "I had to dig through a shit-ton of guest mail to find it."

"I do," I say sincerely. I get up and take the check out of his hands. He stands aside so I can make it past him, out the door and into the garage.

"Jared?" he calls after me.

I turn.

"You know you can come to me, right? If you need help?" The look on his face is one of fatherly concern and I think again about my own parents. But things are finally turning around. This will be done. I'll be able to go to them soon.

"Thanks, Andy," is all I say.

I hobble into the bar to see if Jessie is working. It isn't "officially" open yet, but I can hear movement in the kitchen and Jessie's voice calling to the cook. The lights are off, but the sun reflecting off the lake pours through the windows, making the walls shimmer and dance. She comes out the swinging door carrying a basket of what looks like carnival food— a hamburger, crinkle cut fries, and a full pickle.

She stops when she sees me, studying my face. I can't read her reaction. Concern? Pity? Frustration? She slides her plate across the bar to the seat next to me. "Pepsi?" she says, filling a glass with ice and starting the soda flowing.

"Mountain Dew?"

She nods, grabs another glass and fills it with lime-green caffeine and sugar.

"Stop eating my fries." She slides on to the stool next to me and hands me my drink.

"Sorry, I thought you were giving it to me."

She purposefully eats a fry, crinkle by crinkle, with her front teeth. Like a beaver. When it's all the way in her mouth she smiles. "This is my only meal today. I'm hungry."

"Me too." I steal another fry and she puts the basket further away from me and throws an elbow out. I double over, gasping. When I can breathe, I try to laugh it off.

"Oh my God, I'm sorry, I didn't mean to—"

"It's okay," I say.

"Do you want me to see if Fred will make you something?"

I shake my head. No money.

She slides the basket over and lets me steal a few more fries. "Heard you got fired."

I nod.

"Why?"

"Missed too many days of work."

"Before or after whatever is going on here?" She waves her hand, indicating my body in general.

"After this," I point to my nose, "but before this," I point to my crutches.

"Ouch, not all one accident?"

I shake my head.

"You've got to be the most unlucky son of a bitch I've ever met. What happened?"

"ATV accident," I say. It's easier if I tell everyone the same lie. "And Eric and I were out scouting for deer yesterday. I tripped."

She cringes in sympathy, but continues to eat. "What're you going to do now?"

"I think I'm going to take off. I need to get out of town. I never intended to be here this long."

"What brought you here in the first place? I never did hear your story."

I shrug. "I thought it would be cool for a summer. A friend of mine used to spend weekends here with his family." It was nice not to have to make up another lie. I'm glad I never mentioned the possibility of going to school to her. Andy was the only one who knew that was my "plan."

"Where are you headed?"

"I don't know. I want to go back home, but I'm not sure if my parents will let me. Plus, if I show up like this, they'll think I'm just coming for sympathy."

Last Christmas's voicemail is still burned into my memory: *We love you and we always will. There will always be a place for you to come home to, but we cannot have you bring the gambling or the drugs with you. You know where to find us when you are ready.*

"You and your parents close?" Jessie pulls me back to the present.

"We used to be."

"What happened?"

"Life."

"Bad divorce? Evil step-whatever?"

I shake my head. "No. My life, not theirs."

She nods. "Well, other than this," she gestures with her head, "it seems to me like you're getting it together. You should call them." She slides off the stool and uses her tongue to clean her teeth. "But break up with Kelly first. You don't want to bring crazy like that home, or they'll never let you in the door."

I laugh. "You're right."

"Give me a hug. I've got to get to work. Stop by before you leave town— you're not leaving right now are you?"

"No, at least a few more days."

She nods.

"Well, then give me a hug now, and another one on your way out of town."

I happily oblige and let her hold me just a minute longer than simple friends. If it weren't for Kelly, and if I weren't here just to make money, Jessie is someone I could have really been with.

****

At home I cut the museum address out of a brochure I grabbed before leaving the lodge. I tape it to my envelope, and tape the envelope shut. It's crumpled, but I don't think it'll take away from the impact.

I put the note in the outgoing mailbox in the hallway.

And wait.

I have three days.

Why did I say Monday, not Saturday or Sunday?

Shit! Why didn't I use gloves? My fingerprints are all over that envelope and letter. I was so smart about the robbery– I've got to get the letter back. I open the mail chute and try to stick my hand in, but it's too small. There has to be a way to take the door off completely in case someone gets an envelope stuck. I try wiggling it back and forth, but there doesn't seem to be an easy way to remove it. I open and close it as hard as I can, trying to break it off. I let my crutches drop so I can grip it with both hands and try to rip it to the side.

It stays firmly attached and I lose my balance and fall sideways on the floor. My hands are bleeding, cut by the metal lip on the door. I pull myself up to start back into my apartment, but instead I swing the crutch as hard as I can at the mailbox. I connect and the middle crumples. I grab it again, but instead of coming off in my hands, it doesn't move at all. I swing again, wishing I had a baseball bat instead of a crutch. Nothing loosens the fucking door. I want to scream, but instead throw my crutch as hard as I can and stand there, trying to catch my breath.

I calm down and realize I have to get the crutch back in order to get back to my apartment.

I use the wall for support, but I can't keep all of the weight off my broken leg as I hobble down the hallway for the second crutch. The pain shots through my ankle and out my eyes in bright bursts. I can't see anything else.

My phone rings but I don't answer it. Back in my apartment, I listen to Kelly's voicemail. She got screwed over and her weekend work schedule has been changed. "I'll try to come over, but they've got me closing tonight and doing doubles both tomorrow and Sunday."

I'm glad I didn't have to pretend to be disappointed. Eric calls.

"I need my fucking pain pills. I have a broken fucking leg," I say when I answer the phone.

He just laughs.

I hang up on him. The pharmacy already told me they can't refill for two weeks.

I get some ice from the freezer and strap it around my leg as best I can and try to sleep. But the pain is too intense. I'm sweaty and smell bad. There must have been something in the dust in that mine. Maybe now, since I'm already on the verge of blacking out from the pain, is the best time to shower. Get all the pain out of the way, and then just sleep. Hopefully until Monday.

I sit on the toilet to take the boot off. My ankle is a disgusting shade of greenish-purple with red and brown splotches. I try to stand up and pee, but I keep losing balance and putting my toes down which sends jolts of pain through my leg and out my eyes. There's no way I'm going to be able to stand in the shower.

I look at the tub— I've never really cleaned it out— and decide that it's still better than trying to stand in the shower. The thought of a bath makes me feel both like a kid— which is the last time I took a bath— and a jerk that I would make fun of.

How was your baaath?

Did you have bubbles?

I rinse the tub out so it's a little bit cleaner, and fill it. When I lower myself into the water, a little too hot for the summer day, I feel my body relax. I keep my ankle propped up as much as I can, conscious that the warm water and the angle will encourage swelling. I don't soak long, but feel immensely better and cleaner when

I get out. I bounce, naked, to my room, get dressed, and go back to the bathroom for the boot. By the time I'm done and the water has drained, I lie down and let the exhaustion overtake the pain.

*****

I spend most of the day on Saturday lying on the couch in my apartment watching TV. I ignore the phone and let it go to voicemail. Joey. Eric. Kelly. Twice. I wonder if she knows I'm on to her and Eric. I drift in and out of sleep, wake up starving and order a pizza. I apologize to the delivery kid— I don't have any extra cash for a tip. It makes me feel like a total jackass, but it's not a lie. I know there is a little bit of a buffer left on the credit card, but it's close to maxed out. I need to keep it for an emergency. And at some point Joey is going to have to pay the bill, and then he'll call me and remind me the balance of my tab. And that it won't stay open indefinitely.

Charles calls. I let it go to voicemail twice but answer the third time. I don't need to piss him off any more than he already is.

"Where you been?" he asks.

"Taking care of things."

"Heard you got hurt?"

I don't know what to say. I can't tell what kind of trap he's laying or how he would know about my ankle. I think for a moment and then realize maybe he's talking about my nose and ribs. What *he* did. I have to decide whether to play it down— it is really the least of my worries right now— or make him think it really made an impression on me. I settle on vagueness. "Yeah, life's kinda rough right now."

"You got my money?"

"Not yet, but I do have a plan."

"A *plan?*"

"Yeah."

"Is this like the first plan you had? The one that ended up with a dead buyer and you with the hottest shoes in the world?"

I take a deep breath. It is a lot like that plan, actually. And I don't know how much I want to tell him. The less anyone knows, the better. I've got to start doing this right. "It's a better plan."

"You sure?"

"I'm sure."

"So if I come over say, tomorrow, you gonna have some money to give me?"

"Not tomorrow. Monday." I reconsider very quickly and add, "Tuesday. Tuesday would be better."

He laughs his bitter laugh. "I'm glad you can fit me into your schedule on Tuesday. Why can't I come tomorrow?"

"Banker's hours," is the best I can come up with.

He likes it though, and he laughs. "Alright, I like it when the bank gets involved. They definitely have money. Tuesday it is, then. I'm not bringing you coffee, either."

I sit on the couch and let *Law & Order* reruns play. I'm watching them, but not really, thinking about how my life might soon become an episode. The commercials for the ten o'clock news include teasers about the Slippers, but I don't think much of it.

Until the news starts.

"Breaking news out of Grand Rapids tonight. Police are saying they have been contacted by the thief of the Slippers."

I'm not sure if this is good or not. Why would they go directly to the media?

"Lisa has the story."

"Thanks Paul. Police are saying The Judy Garland Museum received a ransom letter today. The thief is demanding half a million dollars in exchange for the Slippers' return."

Officer Cox appears on the screen. *"We're still working to authenticate the letter. Normally we don't negotiate with criminals, but in this situation, since there are no actual lives in danger, our highest priority is getting the Slippers home safely."*

"Paul, we'll continue to follow any developments in this case. Back to you."

I am sitting on the edge of the couch. I let out a long, relieved exhale. It sounds like they are going to work with me. I struggle to standing and hobble into the kitchen. I need to move around. But I need to stay in my apartment, continue to lay low. I can't go out, because I can't let the cops think I am celebrating. They might be laying a trap.

I hope Kelly hasn't seen the news. They sometimes play it at the bar in Applebee's, but not usually on the weekends. I wonder if Eric has seen it. Maybe he's there, waiting for Kelly to get off work. She'll be done around eleven.

I am so relieved, I don't even care.

*****

I wake up Sunday morning and hobble/run into the bathroom, without my crutches. I barely make it before the vomiting starts. My ribs and ankle are screaming and the pain sends another wave of nausea through my body. I didn't eat much last night, but I'm glad I ate at all. At least I'm not dry heaving again.

I sit on the side of the tub with my head resting against the wall. I have a fever; I can feel it, but I have no idea how hot I am. I must drift off, because the light is different when I open my eyes again. I have to get back into my room, get back to my crutches, before I can do anything else. Heat pulses in my ankle. I hop, steadying myself against the wall, thankful the store is closed, and no one is under me. By the time I've got my crutches I have to go right back in the bathroom to puke again.

I spend most of the day back and forth from the couch to the bathroom, barely registering the Sunday news shows that are recapping the horror in New Orleans. At one point I wake up to some car race. My phone rings, but it's in the bedroom and I'm on the couch. I make a mental note to get it the next time I get up, since my stomach is grumbling and I feel like I'll be in the bathroom again soon, but then I'm asleep again.

I wake up a few times in the dark.

Then light is coming in the window. The person on TV says it's Monday.

I force myself up. I need to get ready to call the museum.

*****

I'm glad I didn't set a morning time for the call. I'm still feverish, wrapped in blankets and shivering. My foot feels like it's on fire. I try to ignore it. I make myself get up and move around. My stomach convulses as I hang my head over the toilet. I haven't eaten, though, so nothing comes up. I need someone. I have messages from Kelly and Eric, but I really want to call Jessie. I don't. I can't get her involved. I care about her too much. I force myself to drink a glass of water before I set an alarm on my phone and lie back down on the couch. I drift in and out of consciousness without really sleeping. I dream about Kelly as The Wicked Witch and Charles as one of the Flying Monkeys.

When the alarm goes off at twelve-thirty I struggle to get my eyes open. I feel like I'm swimming and can't get to the surface. It's hard to breathe. The air cast is much tighter around my leg than it should be.

All I want to do is go back to sleep.

Instead, I go to the kitchen table.

At one o'clock exactly I dial the number.

"Judy Garland Museum, how can I help you?"

"I need to talk to someone about the Slippers." I had meant to disguise my voice, speak lower and clipped, like a robot, but instead it sounds wheezy and shallow. Either way, at least it doesn't sound like me.

"This is John, I'm the Executive Director. How can I help you?"

"John. Did you get my note?"

"Do you have the Slippers?"

"Do you have my money?"

"Are the shoes safe?

"Do you have my money?"

He hesitates and I think I can hear other people whispering, but I can't tell for sure if it's real or if it's the fever. I think I might faint. I prop my head on my hand.

"Sir, I'm sorry, we can't pay you. We don't have that kind of money."

"Don't fucking lie to me."

"I'm sorry."

"What about the insurance?" I know I should hang up, I know I've been on too long and they will have traced the call by now. But I'm desperate. I have to get the money.

"We don't have insurance. The man who owns the Slippers, he has insurance."

"WELL THEN LET ME TALK TO HIM!" I scream. I think I'm going to cry. I can't cry.

"He's not here. He lives in California." John's voice is calm, soothing, like he feels sorry for me. "I really wish— I mean, we want the shoes back more than anything. If I could give you the money—"

"How much do you have?"

"How much?"

"How much can you come up with? Today? How much if I return the shoes today?"

"I don't know— I would have to—"

"HOW MUCH?"

"Forty-five, maybe fifty thousand?

"That's not enough."

I hang up.

*****

Shit shit shit shit shit! How could I have been so stupid? I sent the fucking ransom note to the wrong person? How is that even possible?

I call Eric. "We're fucked, man. The money— the museum—" I'm having a hard time speaking, I feel like I'm choking. "There's no money. They don't have insurance—"

That's the last thing I remember.

TWENTY

It doesn't take long for the police to trace the call, or arrive at Jared's door. They knock, they yell, and then they kick the door down.

Officer Richards is the first through the door. "He's over here!" he yells. "Jared Canning, you are under arrest. Put your hands up."

Jared's hands, splayed on the table on either side of his head, don't move. Other than a small shudder, Jared stays completely still.

"Jared?" Officer Cox walks slowly around the far side of the table, his gun trained on Jared, while Richards approaches him from the side. Several other cops follow them in, fill the apartment.

"Jared! Wake up!" Richards hits Jared on the shoulder, a little harder than is necessary. The shoulder jerks in response to the blow, but there is no movement in Jared's face.

Cox puts his gun down and reaches across the table, putting his hand in front of Jared's nostrils. "He's barely breathing," Cox says.

Richards quickly stows his gun too and puts two fingers to Jared's neck.

"Call an ambulance."

*****

Richards stays with Jared while Cox and the rest of the police begin searching the house. They are systematic, thorough, and messy.

The paramedics arrive and lay Jared on the gurney.

"Holy shit, what is that smell?" one of them asks.

Richards shrugs. He assumed it was the way Jared's apartment always smelled. He's learned that most criminals are not very hygienic. They all seem to smell of dirt and booze and weed, and, more often than not, sweat and body odor.

One paramedic listens to Jared's heart and lungs and shouts a list of directions. Soon there is an IV being inserted, a telescopic pole shooting up from the end of the bed to hang it from.

"This foot is green," the other paramedic says as he carefully removes the air cast. The room is filled with a stench so bad everyone takes a step back. Richards gags.

"Holy fuck. What is that?"

"It's infected. Badly." The paramedic is trying to breathe through his mouth, to keep the smell out of his nostrils, but otherwise seems unfazed. "We've got to get him to the hospital, now."

"He's under arrest. We need to talk to him as soon as he wakes up," Cox says, walking with the gurney to the door.

"Honestly," the paramedic says, "I'm not sure if he's going to wake up."

*****

The apartment search reveals nothing other than the empty Vicodin bottle. No one could have taken that many at one time and not died. Cox and Richards agree that he must have sold them. In his truck, they find a cup of red sequins. That's all the confirmation they need. He had the Slippers. Now they just have to figure out where he put them.

Eric arrives later in the afternoon, sees all of the police cars, and leaves. He tries Jared's cell.

"May I help you?" Office Cox answers it.

"Um, hi, is Jared there?"

"No. Who is this?"

"A friend. I was just calling—" Eric fades his voice out, pretends to drop the call.

TWENTY-ONE

I wake up and Charles is standing over me. I panic and try to run, but can't. My arms are strapped to the bed. My legs won't move.

"Shhh," he says, patting my shoulder.

I look around and register the beeping, the tubes, the weight at the end of my leg.

"Calm down or you're going to scare the nurses." Charles looks through the glass wall, obscured by a half-drawn beige curtain, at the one brown-haired woman sitting at a computer, drinking coffee. When she doesn't look our way, he casually walks over and pulls the curtain the rest of the way closed.

"Don't worry. They won't be concerned. I've been here every day, your devoted brother. I draw the curtain every night, so you can get the rest you need. And I open it every morning so you'll be encouraged to wake up by the movement during the day. I'm so concerned about you."

I want to speak, but I can't. Something is filling my mouth, gagging me. I try to cough

"Oh, yeah, they had to intubate you. For the surgery." He watches my eyes, seeing if I register what he's saying at all. "You really fucked up. Your leg got infected. You didn't go to the doctor like you were supposed to. The infection spread to your lungs pretty quickly. You must have had some sort of lowered immune system. It's really rare, for a simple broken bone to get infected. It usually only happens when you have a compound fracture, or have had surgery. That's some really bad luck you have."

I watch him, terrified of what he's going to do. I sneak my hand toward the nurse-call button, but he sees me.

"Oh, don't bother her. She's busy with other patients. More important patients. What do you need? You want some water? They said you'd be thirsty if you woke." He takes a Styrofoam cup off the side table and pours water out of a plastic pitcher, and bends the straw down. I lift my head, forgetting the tubes, trying to reach the straw. Instead of bringing it closer to my face, he pours the cold liquid down my chest.

"Ooops," he laughs. "Sorry about that." He moves the nurse call button away from my hand. "We're done, Jared. You didn't hold up your end of the bargain. And I'm sorry about that, because I really like you. But if I let you get away with this, then everyone will think they can make bets with me they can't cover."

I make a gurgling noise, the most I can get out of my throat.

"No, no, I know what you're thinking. But they will find out. Everyone in the country already knows about the botched ransom note. They know that you stole the Slippers."

He's pacing now. I try to follow him with my gaze, but he's soon out of my line of sight. I press the button to raise the head of the bed. That helps a bit, but he's at my side within seconds putting it back down.

"No, no, no. You can't do that. The nurses might realize you're awake and come see how you are. We're not ready for them yet. We're *talking*."

He continues to pace. I can't turn my head to really look at him. He seems nervous, but I can't tell if it's just wishful thinking on my part. If he's nervous, maybe he won't go through with it.

I wonder if he's ever gone through with it. He continues to walk around the room, talking, mostly to himself it seems, random mumblings under his breath that I can't really hear over the noise of the respirator. I want this thing out of my throat so badly. I pull lightly at my restraints, not enough to draw attention to myself, but just trying to see if there is any play — any way I could undo them myself without Charles noticing. They are soft cuffs with hook and loop tabs. It looks like maybe, if I can hook the end of the tab on the bed's side rail, I could rip them off. But not without Charles hearing.

He looks over at me and I slide my hand back down, keeping my eyes on his.

"Do you understand what I'm saying?" he asks, standing over top of me again.

I don't move. I have no idea what he was saying. And a wrong answer might be worse than no answer at all. My mouth hurts from the tubes going into my throat. My eyes are watering. I blink several times, trying to clear them. The respirator and other sounds are deafening.

"You can't hear me?" Charles asks, suddenly caring. "It's loud over here, isn't it? You probably can't hear me." He leans in, close to my ear. I feel tension on the tube in my throat and the tape holding it to my face. My head comes up. He notices and smiles, but moves and the tension releases. "I said," he whispers, "Not to worry. No one will ever know about me. They'll think the infection was just too much for your lungs. I do wish you could talk, tell me where the shoes are. But I'll find them on my own. Your friends, they're not too smart. That Kelly, she likes to talk. I'll start with her."

He smiles, grabs the tubes and gives one hard pull. There's searing pain as the tape rips off my face. I can't breathe. My entire body is being turned inside out. The machines go crazy, a fire drill of alarms and sirens. He quickly unstraps one of my hands and stands back, watching. I flail, trying to pull the tubes the rest of the way out, trying to unstrap my other hand, coughing, choking...

Drowning.

TWENTY-TWO

Eric noticed the new truck at the corner of the street when he pulled up, but he didn't think much of it. People around here bought new trucks all the time, with money they didn't have. They'd drive them around for a few months, treat them like shit, and not put up a fight when the repo man came. It was a game.

The cop cars were still at Jared's, but Eric had a plan. He knew a few of the guys on the force. He would just go in, pretend he was just curious, and see what he could find out. He needed to know if Jared had said anything about the mine. More than anything, he didn't want the shoes found on his grandparents' property. Almost anything. He didn't want to get in trouble either.

He parked and was half way up to the building's front door when Kelly came out in handcuffs. He stopped and backed away, trying not to be too noticeable, but trying to catch her eyes. The cop leading her was Alan— he'd been friends with Eric's dad since Eric was a kid. Kelly had her head down, her long hair falling in front of her face. She was wearing a pink tank top with a red bra under it and Daisy-Duke cutoffs that showed a little bit of her ass with each step she took. He felt a wave of jealousy go through him. Why was she wearing that to visit Jared? She was supposed to be breaking up with him.

Eric clenched and unclenched his fist and let his body turn and track her to the police car. She put her head up for just a moment while they slid her in the back seat. Her eyes were puffy and red, there were tears streaking down her cheeks.

Their eyes locked. "He's dead," she said. The door closed and the police officers turned to look at him.

"He's dead?" Eric asked.

Alan turned and saw him for the first time. "Hey Eric, what are you doing here?"

"She's my girlfriend. I mean friend. I mean, she's my friend's girlfriend"

The officers exchanged a glance. "This is Tom's son," Alan said to the man standing next to him. "This is Officer Cox."

Eric nodded. "What did she mean? Who's dead? Jared? How?" Eric said.

"Do you know Jared Canning?" Cox asked.

"Yes. I mean, no." He ran a hand through his hair and looked at the ground. "I mean, I don't know him well."

"Would you be willing to answer a few questions?"

"About what? What's going on? I mean, I know Jared was in trouble..." *Shut up!* Eric screamed at himself. He was scared. He was talking too much. Did he hear Kelly correctly? He couldn't have. Jared couldn't be dead.

"Sir, this is the site of an ongoing investigation—" Cox began.

"Eric's a good kid. He's not involved in this," Alan interrupted.

Cox ignored him. "If you know the people involved," he said to Eric, "You could really help us out by answering a few questions."

"Okay," Eric said, tentatively. "But I'd like to talk to Jared first."

"I'm sorry, sir, that can't happen."

"Well, can I at least see him?"

"How are you acquainted with Mr. Canning?"

"We're friends. I mean—"

"I'm sorry, Eric," Alan said. "Mr. Canning died this afternoon."

Eric backpedaled. "He what?"

"I'm sorry." Alan said. "But it really would be helpful if you could come to the station with us to answer a few questions. We're having a hard time getting in touch with his family. Any information you can give us."

"What's happening with Kelly? Why's she being arrested?"

"She's just going to be held for a little while. She's— I'm sure she's just upset, but she's trying to keep us from doing our jobs. She's being charged with interfering in an investigation, but I'm sure once she calms down...she's just kind of hysterical right now."

Eric swallowed and nodded. "I've got to get to work right now," he said. "Would it be okay if I came out later?"

Cox started to say something, but Alan interrupted him. "The sooner the better."

"I can probably get out in three, four hours, tops."

Alan nodded. "We appreciate it. What about her? Do you know someone we could call to sit with her?"

"Her mom. She lives over by the college. Her number is in Kelly's cell phone."

TWENTY-THREE

Eric tried to walk calmly to his car, but he wanted to run. Once inside, he used all of his restraint to drive at a normal speed down the road. He sped up a little bit when he was about a mile away, and floored it when he hit the edge of town. The forty-mile drive to his grandparents' farm felt like it took hours. He kept checking his cell phone, willing Kelly to call.

He didn't know whether the cops were going to be able to connect him to Jared and the shoes or not. He hadn't told anyone, but he wasn't sure if Jared and Kelly had talked about his involvement. Eric thought he might be in love with her, but he knew better than anyone that Kelly couldn't be trusted. It would've been smart of Jared to tell Kelly about Eric's involvement, because she had been talking so much about the shoes that it would have helped to spread the blame a little. Give the cops two tails to chase instead of just looking at him.

But, then again, Jared was thinking about cutting her off completely. So giving her more information wouldn't have been a logical move.

There was no way to tell. And no way to predict what Kelly would say to the cops, regardless of what she knew. She looked hysterical.

His phone rang. "Are you okay?" he said without looking at it.

"Yeah, babe, I'm fine." Sherrie said. Eric sank back in his seat and rubbed his eyes. "Did you hear? That guy that you hung out with at Jack's sometimes, Jared? He stole the Ruby Slippers. He's dead. He died at the hospital today. They didn't say how. I bet the cops shot him."

"What?" He momentarily forgot how worried he was about Kelly. "Why would they have shot him?"

"I don't know. But they stormed his apartment, and he's dead now. Crazy isn't it? And that *he* stole the Ruby Slippers?"

"Yeah, wow, I had no idea," Eric said. His voice sounded hollow to his own ears. He hoped Sherrie wouldn't notice, or would misinterpret his tone as shock or sadness. "Do they have the shoes now?"

"No! They weren't there! They're saying they are still looking, and asked again for anyone who knows anything to come forward."

Eric let a silent sigh out of his lips. "Listen," he said, "I just got to Grandpa's. I have to run in here for a minute. I'll call you back, okay?"

"Okay."

"Hey," Eric said quickly, "did you hear anything about Kelly?"

"No. Why?"

"No reason. I just heard..." he tried to find words that wouldn't get him in trouble. "I heard that she might have something to do with it too."

"Nope, they didn't say anything about her on the news."

"Huh," he tried to sound uninterested. "Cool. Let me run in here, okay? I'll call you back."

"Okay. I love you!"

"Love you too," he mumbled as he was hanging up.

He parked his car at the edge of his grandparents' property and snuck through the woods. When he got to the stream he crossed it immediately in one long jump, like he'd been doing since he was a kid. When he broke through to the field he sprinted to the mine's door, but stopped at the bottom of the crumbling cement stairs.

Someone had been there.

The door— the old wooden door that had been hanging partially open for all of Eric's life had been replaced. The new door looked like grey steel, was latched, and, he confirmed, was locked. He didn't remember the mine ever being locked before.

He walked around, looking for another opening, dread filling his stomach with every step. Every door had been replaced. The few windows were boarded up with plywood. He knew he could get a crowbar or hammer and get in through one of them, but he wasn't confident he would be able to find his way through the dark maze once inside. He had only ever gone in through the main door.

He reached in his pocket for a flashlight. Nothing. He left it sitting on the passenger seat. He forgot to grab it after talking to Sherrie.

"Whatcha doing out here again?"

The voice made him jump. He turned and watched Brad light a cigarette, then wipe a greasy hand across his forehead.

"When did this get boarded up?"

"Yesterday. Been too many trespassers out here. Cops are getting worried some idiot might try to hide a meth lab inside and blow us all up."

Eric nodded, trying to seem nonchalant. "Who has the key?"

"Who wants to know?" Brad asked.

"Me." Eric said.

"What do you need?"

"I hid some stuff in there when I was a kid. I want to get it back."

"That's what this trip is? Sudden sentimentality?"

Eric shrugged. "I guess."

"What about last week? Why didn't you get it then?"

"I didn't know they were closing it off. I figured I could come back any time I wanted."

"And you decided to come back today?"

Eric was starting to get frustrated, but he couldn't show it. Brad wanted him to get frustrated. It was the same power struggle they'd been in since they were kids and Eric had never understood why. Sometimes, like that night at Jared's, the night Kelly first found the shoes, Brad could be completely cool. But most of the time he was just a dick.

"Why don't you tell me what you need, and where you put it, and I'll go in and get it for you," Brad offered, smiling.

"You have a key?" Eric asked.

Brad nodded once. "I do."

"Can you just let me in, then?"

Brad shook his head. "Sorry, cuz, I can't do that."

"Why?"

"Nobody allowed inside."

"Except you."

"'Cept me."

Eric took a deep breath, refusing to get drawn into the fight. "What I hid is kind of private. You can just let me back in this one time, can't you? That's why they trusted you with the key."

Appealing to his ego seemed to be working. Brad paused, thinking it over. Then his eyes clouded and he shrugged. "Nope, sorry. I'm the only one allowed in or out."

"Does Grandpa know?"

"I told you last time, this isn't his property."

"It might as well be. He was the caretaker here since the mine closed. Maybe I should go ask him."

"You can try. But he doesn't have a key, so it doesn't really matter what he says."

Eric nodded. "If that's the way you're going to be." He started back toward his grandparents' house through the woods, the route he was most comfortable with, while his cousin turned the other way and walked up the road. Eric knew that Brad would probably beat him, but he didn't think Brad would go to their grandfather. Since Brad had moved into their basement a few years earlier, his grandparents seemed to have less patience for his constant bickering with everyone in the community. Eric formulated his plan as he walked and was fairly confident that he would be able to convince his grandfather to intervene (if Grandpa didn't have his own key— Eric couldn't believe that Brad had been designated the sole key holder.) He noticed the truck as he neared the edge of the woods, and it felt a bit familiar, but there were so many Silverados around he ignored the thought.

He knocked on the door as he let himself in. "Hey, Grandpa. You here?" He kicked his shoes off and walked through the entryway into the kitchen, where his Grandfather was sitting at the table with a guy about Eric's age.

"Hi Eric!" Grandpa smiled. "Charles said he was supposed to meet you here. I didn't realize you were coming."

Eric nodded. "Hello," he said. "I'm sorry, I don't remember you— how can I help you?"

Charles smiled and nodded. "No, I'm sorry to barge in on you. I thought we had decided we would meet here—I must have misunderstood."

Eric looked from his grandfather to Charles and back. "Are you a friend of Grandpa's?"

"No, we just met," Grandpa offered. "But he seems like a very nice guy."

"I'm doing some research on the abandoned mines up here," Charles said. "Jared Canning told me I should talk to you. He said you might even be able to offer me a tour. I thought he set up this meeting for us."

"Jared told you to talk to me?" This must be who Jared was fighting with on the phone. Why would he have told him the hiding spot? Eric remembered Jared's "ATV accident." He suddenly remembered that Jared was dead. It was so new, he had forgotten. Charles smiled. Eric wanted to turn around, back out the door and run. But he couldn't. He couldn't leave his grandfather in the same house as this guy.

"I can take you down there," Eric said, "But I can't let you in. They changed the doors and locks recently."

"Oh, don't worry about that," his grandfather said. "Brad's got a key. He can let you in. It's important that we continue to learn about these mines— we need to keep the industry alive, but we need to do it the right way."

"I couldn't agree more," Charles said, standing. "You lead the way."

"Stop in before you leave, okay?" his grandfather called after him.

"Sure thing," Eric said.

*****

They walked silently down the porch and into the yard. When they were out of earshot of the house, Eric turned to Charles. "Who the fuck are you?"

"You have the Slippers?"

"The what?" Eric wasn't sure what to do. He didn't need the money, not like Jared did. He didn't need the shoes. But something was telling him that he couldn't give them to this guy either.

"The *Ruby Slippers*. He gave them to you, didn't he?"

"What did you do to him?"

"Me?" Charles looked shocked, offended. "I didn't do anything to him. He died of a bone infection. Complications of a recent break, I guess."

Eric took an involuntary step back. The cops didn't shoot him.

"Oh, you didn't know?" Charles smiled. "Well, I'm sorry to be the bearer of bad news. Your friend is dead."

Eric swallowed and tried to figure out what he should do. He shouldn't have gotten involved with this. The worst he had ever done was sell a few prescription pain killers. Nothing like this. It was too much.

"So…" Charles said. "The shoes. You hid them for him, didn't you? They're not at his apartment. And Kelly, God bless that ass, she's definitely not smart enough to have hidden them. I mean," he chuckled and leaned toward Eric like they were old friends, "she's so stupid she actually wore them. Lucky for her she is so stupid, though, no one ever took her seriously."

"Shut the fuck up. Leave her out of this."

Charles raised his eyebrows. "Oh— you got something going on there? You hittin' that?"

Eric didn't say anything.

"Well, kudos to you, man," Charles said, clapping him on the back. "I thought you had a pregnant girlfriend. Sherrie, right?"

Eric's choked on his breath. "How do you know that?"

Charles held up his hands. "Hey, no judgment, man. I understand. But, Kelly...I'd be happy to take my turn when you're done with her. Sounds like she gets around enough." His hand moved slightly and he grabbed Eric's shoulder, his thumb digging in under the collarbone enough to hurt. "Listen. I know you have the shoes. You can either get me the shoes, or pay me the money Jared owed me. You decide."

"I don't have the shoes," Eric said, trying not to wince.

"Why did you go to the mine with Jared last week?"

"I didn't."

"How'd he break his ankle then?"

"I don't know."

Charles tightened his grip. Eric gasped. It felt like Charles's thumb was about to separate his shoulder from his body. "Don't fucking lie to me," Charles said, wiggling his thumb deeper. He leaned in and whispered, "This is nothing compared to what Jared felt."

"Everything okay over here?" Brad walked out of the garage. Eric tried to catch his cousin's eyes, willed him to listen to his thoughts.

"Oh, you must be Brad," Charles said, letting go of Eric and approaching, hand out. 'I'm Charles." They gripped hands like old friends. "Your friend here—"

"Cousin," Brad interrupted.

"Cousin," Charles nodded, "offered to give me a tour of the mine a few weeks ago and it's just now worked out for me to get up here. You see, I'm doing some research for the University."

"I've got the key," Brad offered. "I can let you in there. We're just trying to keep the riffraff out," he looked straight at Eric, "but valid research is a completely different situation."

Brad walked over to where his ATV was sitting next to the garage and swung a leg over. "Hop on," he said, standing. "You'll both fit on the back rack."

Charles shrugged and sat on one side, watching Eric.

"You can give the tour," Eric said. "You know the mine better than I do anyway."

"Oh no," Charles said, "I need your perspective. Especially after everything Jared told me."

"I really do know the mine better—"

"It's okay," Charles held a hand up to make Brad stop talking. He pulled up his pants' leg, showing Eric the gun he had holstered near his ankle. "Eric's got a unique perspective I'd like to hear about."

Eric sat down slowly. As soon as he was on, Brad started driving.

"Really, if you're doing research, I would be the best person—"

"I'd rather go in with Eric. Just Eric." Charles cut him off again.

Brad turned and looked at the two of them. Eric knew he was going to protest, he would say that if he didn't go in then no one would go in. Charles wouldn't want to get another person involved. They would all have to go back. Or pretend to explore the mine and leave it at that. Eric had very rarely in his life even liked his cousin, but now he was thanking God for him.

They pulled up next to the door. "I'm really sorry, but if I don't go in, I can't let the two of you in," Brad said as he shut the ATV off and stood up.

"Well, I'm sorry too," Charles said. "I was starting to like you."

It felt like slow motion as Eric watched Charles reach down and pretended to scratch his ankle. The gun came out of the holster just before Charles pulled the trigger. Eric yelled "No!" and registered the look in Brad's eyes just before he heard the explosion. Brad's body jerked backwards, spinning on one leg before he fell next to the four-wheeler.

Charles walked over and dug a set of keys out of Brad's front pocket and tossed them to Eric, pointing the gun at him. "Shall we go in?"

Eric could feel the warmth of Brad's body still on the keys. He couldn't get breath into his lungs. He watched the puddle of blood growing on Brad's T-shirt and starting to spread out under his body, and vomited all over the back of the four wheeler.

"Come on, man, we've still got to ride that back," Charles said. "What's your problem? It didn't seem like you really liked him anyway."

"You didn't have to kill him!" Eric was embarrassed that he was crying. "You could have just—"

"What? Talked him into letting me in? That wasn't working so well for you earlier, was it?"

"I just—"

"Shut the fuck up and open the door," Charles said, pointing the gun at Eric.

The world was tilting, Eric was afraid he was going to pass out. He fumbled and dropped the keys, picked them up, tried again. "I don't know which key—"

"Try them until you find the right one then," Charles said. The absolute calm in his voice brought the bile up in Eric's stomach again and he leaned over the rail and threw up. He wondered what it had been like for Jared. If he knew he was going to die, or if Charles had snuck up on him.

Eric wanted to run. But he knew the gun would catch him. And even if he did get away, Charles would go for his grandparents. Eric kept thinking that maybe, just maybe, once he had the shoes, Charles would go, leave the rest of them alone. He wiped his palms on his pants, tried to steady the shaking, and fit another key in the new deadbolt. This time, it turned. He tried the same key in the doorknob, but it didn't work. He jumped ahead on the ring to another similar key and tried it, and the door swung open.

"Do you have a flashlight?" Eric asked.

"Nope. Do you?"

"No. It's going to be pretty dark—"

"I'm not afraid of the dark," Charles said. "I hear you know this place inside and out."

Eric froze. Would Jared have really told Charles about him? About the mine? He must have. How else could Charles have known?"

"Let's go." Charles said, pushing Eric through the door. Eric stumbled and caught himself just short of tumbling down the metal stairs. Charles laughed. "Be careful," he said. "It's not time for you to die just yet."

Just yet echoed around them in the mine.

"Make sure the door stays open," Eric said, trying to ignore the echo. "We need the light."

Charles nodded and grabbed a broken piece of concrete from the stairs and used it to block the door open. He followed Eric closely enough that Eric could feel Charles's warm breath on the back of his neck.

He retraced the steps he had taken so many times before, walking past the first two passageways and turning into the third. Three steps in, it was complete darkness; Eric couldn't see his own hands. After a dozen or so more steps, he started to feel along the top ledge of the wall, hoping his instincts were right and he was close. He was starting to panic, worried maybe he was in the wrong tunnel, the darkness completely disorienting. He took a few more steps, walking more quickly, deeper into the tunnel. His boot connected with something and he tripped. A tinny thud echoed through the cave. He reached down and picked up the lunchbox. It was open. And empty.

"What is it?" Charles asked.

"It's— it should be right here," Eric said, groping. Finally, he found the recess in the wall. He poked his hand through the sticky hair of a spider web and swept his arm from side to side. There was only dead air, rocks and bugs. He jumped a few times, trying to reach further back, wondering if his hiding place was a deeper crevice than he thought. He wished again for a flashlight.

"They're not," he was breathing hard, both from exertion and terror. "Here. They're gone. I don't—"

"Don't fuck with me," Charles said.

"I'm not fucking with you. This is where we put them. They're—" He realized. "Fucking Brad. He fucking moved them."

"Where would he have put them?" Charles asked.

"How the hell would I know? Brad was a freak. And now you've fucking killed him." Eric started to panic, choking on his words, on the darkness, on the dust. He was turned around. "I've got to get out of here." He ran toward what he thought was the mouth of the tunnel, but Charles caught him easily with one hand.

"Hell no. Not until you find the shoes."

"I can't find the shoes!" Eric screamed. "I don't know where they are! They were here, and now they're gone, and you killed Brad and he's the only one—"

He saw a burst of light before he heard the sound. He was knocked backward, his ears ringing, everything tilting. He didn't fall all the way over—the side of the tunnel held him up. There was a warmth coming from the side of his head, filling his ear, down to his neck.

The last thing he remembered was wondering if Charles would find his way out of the mine or get turned the wrong way in one of the tunnels. Then he closed his eyes.

AUTHOR'S NOTE

Some of the things that happened in this book are real, but most of it is made up. Just so there is no confusion, here's what's real:

On August 25, 2005, sometime after 2:00 am, someone broke the window on the emergency exit at The Judy Garland Museum in Grand Rapids, Minnesota, and stole a pair of shoes, known as The Ruby Slippers, that had been worn by Judy Garland in *The Wizard of Oz*. A single sequin was the only evidence found at the scene.

On August 26, 2005, Hurricane Katrina made landfall in New Orleans, Louisiana, causing catastrophic damage and flooding. The theft of the Ruby Slippers was reported on national news as having happened in Grand Rapids, Michigan.

On August 30, the storm, which had followed a path up through Mississippi, was downgraded to a tropical depression about an hour north of Nashville, TN.

Descriptions of the shoes were recreated using pictures found on the Internet. Descriptions of the museum were based on visits to the museum and help from its director.

The shoes have never been found.

Grand Rapids, Minnesota, is a real place. The Judy Garland Museum, Country Inn, Sawmill Inn, Applebee's, Country Kitchen and Ruttger's are all real places in Grand Rapids.

All of the people are fake, complete figments of my imagination, except two: The Executive Director of the Judy Garland Museum is really named John. And the Ruby Slippers were really owned by Michael Shaw.

Acknowledgments

Thank you to everyone who worked on this book, who helped me make it happen. To John Kelsch at the Judy Garland Museum for giving me access to the museum for research and for helping with the actual details of the theft. To Mom, for being my first reader and editor, not just for this piece, but for everything I've ever written (did you see that? I didn't say everything that I've ever written. I'm learning!) To Leigh and Ashley for your early reading and editing. To Jessica at Rare Bird Editing for making the actual editing process so much better than I ever could have imagined. Thank you for your patience, insight and diligence. To Chris Tobias for making my cover amazing. Thank you to Joe

Hart and Ben Barnhart for helping me navigate the self-publishing world.

To my mentors: Jan Ferraro, Angie Ulseth, Loren Brown, Linda Busby-Parker and Charlotte Rains Dixon, thank you for teaching me how to read like a writer, how to get words on the page, and how to arrange them in an intriguing way.

To my family: I am truly blessed to have all of you. I can't name you all here, because, well, there are too many of you. You know who you are. Mom and Dad, thank you for your constant, continued support. Chris, Lily and Austin: you are my favorites. Thank you for understanding I need to write and giving me the time and space to make it happen.

About the Author

Amanda Michelle Moon writes books inspired by real events. Her first two novels, The Thief and The Damage, tell the true-life unsolved mystery of a pair of Wizard of Oz worn ruby slippers from the perspective first of a fictional criminal, and then of the people affected by the theft. Both books can be found at www.stealingtherubyslippers.com. When she's not writing, she lives with her family in Minneapolis, Minnesota, and works for NoiseTrade Books. Connect with her and find out about her works-in-progress at amandamichellemoon.com.

Made in the USA
Middletown, DE
10 May 2015